The Pilgrimage of Piltdown Man

The Pilgrimage of Piltdown Man

Mike O'Leary

Published by:
Triarchy Press
Axminster, England

info@triarchypress.net
www.triarchypress.net

A catalogue record is available from the British Library.

Cover illustration: Renate Debrun - www.renatedebrun.com

Print ISBN: 978-1-911193-57-9

ePub ISBN: 978-1-911193-58-6

To all those who resist the A27 smashing through Binsted and Knuckeridoodle land, and to all those liable to resist the by-pass to a by-pass, an offshoot of the M27, smashing through the inner city of Southampton.

To Edward Thomas's Lob, who keeps clear the paths that no-one ever uses.

The Pilgrimage of Piltdown Man

1 Piltdown
2 Tunbridge Wells
3 Nan Tuck's Lane
4 The Devil's Dyke
5 Bramber Castle / Steyning
6 Chanklebury
7 Amberley Wild Brooks
8 Whiteways Roundabout
9 The Lyminster Knuckerhole
10 The Binsted Knuckerhole
11 Farlington Marshes
12 Swanwick Air Traffic Control
13 Millstone Marshes, Northam
14 Hag Hill
15 Burley Beacon
16 Amesbury
17 Adam's Grave
18 Priddy
19 Glastonbury Tor
20 Somerset Levels
21 Bridgwater Services
22 Yes Tor
23 Wistman's Wood
24 Brent Tor
25 Dozmary Pool
26 Cornwall Services
27 Trecrobben
28 Zennor

Ys/Lyonesse

Widdershins around the Menez Bré

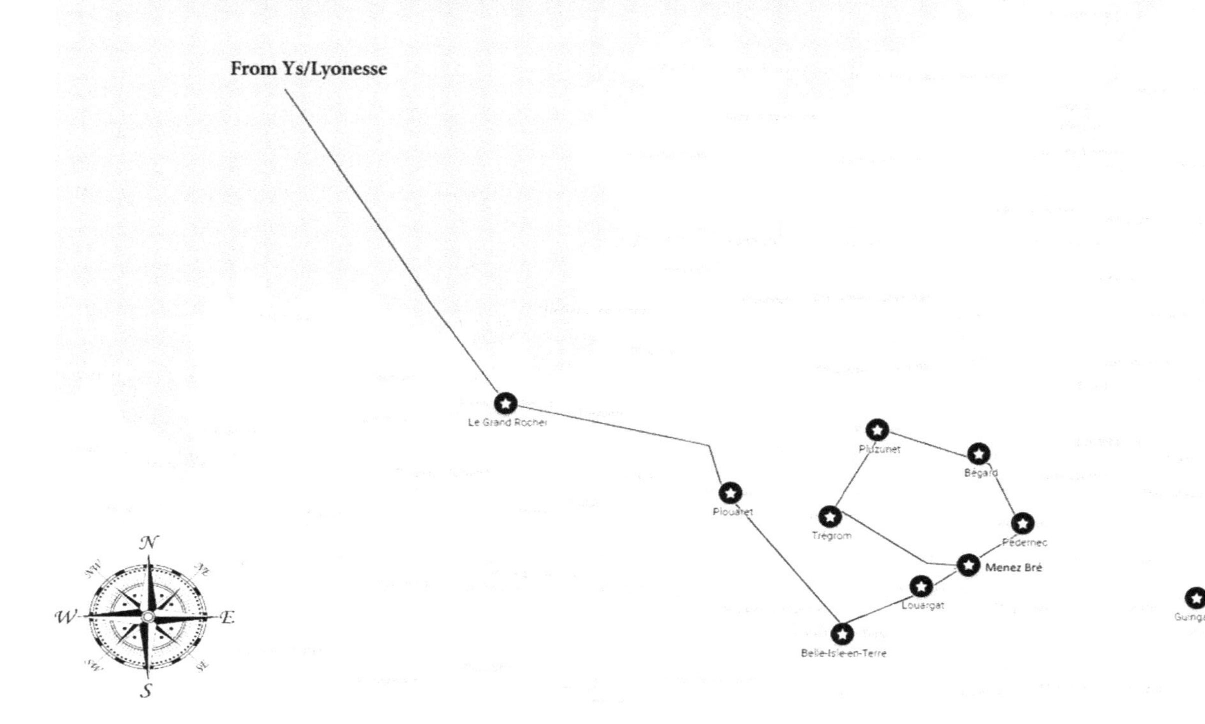

Contents

Foreword

The old stories are powerful things. Used malevolently to misrepresent, demonise and scapegoat, they cause substantial damage in people's lives. This is generally well known. What is far less often recognised – and what makes this book such a special piece of storytelling – is that there is another kind of potency in these tales. This lies less with their satirical or even fantastic qualities – the weird and the eerie – but more with the materiality of their contents. Their vibrancy is both an inspiration and a threat to readers and tellers. Invoke the old stories lightly or credulously, and you may find the characters have joined you in ways that are not always easy to live with. Fortunately, we are in safe, grubby and experienced hands with Mike O'Leary.

This possibility of entanglement is reciprocal. The old stories are just as vulnerable to us as we are to them. When we neglect them, their characters fade and move beyond our understanding; they lose a grip on their own liveableness when they pass beyond the range of our senses. Ignore the characters – Old Nan, Lord Moon, the mysterious Breton, Jenny Greenteeth – and we lose them from our shared, and thus shrinking, world. Equally, when we turn them into light entertainment, jokes or adventure commodities, we constitute a danger both to the stories and to ourselves. For these are the stories of ecologies with weird consciousness, of hybrid and mutant portents of the future, and of the spooks of our own desires that we humans need in order to draw ourselves back from the mutual destruction of mind and matter. When we do violence to our folktales we do violence to folk. As the Mermaid of Zennor says: "you reach into a story, you hack at a story, you change it. The story isn't just something outside yourself."

But it is outside, also. The stories of *Piltdown Man* are tangible things, made upon shifting geologies, from chalks and sandstones. In their irreducible scuzziness, the tales and their characters repeatedly lay claim to specific places in a grainy world and re-enchant by a dirty and improvised magic. There are no esoteric systems in this book. Transformations have to be improvised; there is no transcendence from the hard surface of the road, only a sinking into loam, or a sidetrack into a mermaid's watery domain. Such queer specificities – from the jumbled wing, claw, pink trainers and possible beak of the book's central character, Link, to the unreliable earthiness of the floors of forests and laybys through which Link descends to converse with 'the others' – are locked in struggle with a monoculture that seeks to build the same everywhere. O'Leary is on the side of the stories; he throws out all homogeneity, serving up startling changes of scale, tone and direction, switching from "internal ecstasy to a fight with a group of squaddies" at the turn of a page. Yet, at the same time he weaves so fine and rich a web of tales that the reader is supported from start to finish, even as the tales' deterritorialisations stretch out of the page and into the roots in our chests.

The central character of Link – a figure made up from bit parts, like Mary Shelley's monster – is the dynamo here. He links. His indiscriminate woundedness and openness – qualities that leave him battered – allow his journey to thicken, grow hairier and, through unrealness, to flood the real. No boundary is fixed in, or by, this book. If a character reappears then they are tweaked by their change of location; the devil in Dartmoor is not the same devil as he was in Tunbridge Wells. Tone is unpredictable; in a book as enchanting as this intends to be, nothing quite prepares us for as uncomfortable a scene as when Link – tramp/crow/mortuary mash-up – finds himself walking in pink trainers, female and teenage and suffers the shrinking space of a car's back seat. Until "a wing encircled the young man, there was a face of scars and stitches, there was fur and feathers – a wriggling of insects. The young man forgot to scream as the wing started to squeeze and snap his ribs..."

A master of unstitching assumptions, O'Leary does the business on his own creation (and himself), shredding explanations, until, for a while, all that retains tangibility is the path of the quest itself, and even that – "not knowing what was an abbey and what was a supermarket" – is faint. Yet, the route, the grounds of travel, is somehow enough to bring us by exhausting ambulatory quest from Kent via the West Country (with occasional dragon flights) to Brittany where O'Leary prepares for a final pulling of the rug from under his own feet. Old stories that are so often dragged out for the purposes of solidifying – in weak nationalist cultural nostalgia, or as set dressing for foundational or essentialist narratives – are liberated here; *Piltdown Man* gobs all that conservatism away in a rough embrace of filthy magic, glorious revenge upon mind-crushing saints and an invitation to its readers to take the risk and ask the 'old characters' of the earth to power up again in their imaginations.

Phil Smith

1: THE PILTDOWN MAN

Cryptid: An animal whose existence or survival is disputed or unsubstantiated, such as the yeti.

Oxford English Dictionary

The Weald: The Weald /ˈwiːld/ is an area in South East England situated between the parallel chalk escarpments of the North and the South Downs. It crosses the counties of Sussex, Hampshire, Kent and Surrey. It has three separate parts: the sandstone 'High Weald' in the centre; the clay 'Low Weald' periphery; and the Greensand Ridge, which stretches around the north and west of the Weald and includes its highest points. The Weald once was covered with forest, and its name, Old English in origin, signifies *woodland.* The term is still used today, as scattered farms and villages sometimes refer to the Weald in their names.

Wikipedia

Once upon a time…

there was the Weald. Much of the Weald was smoke and flame – a place of blast furnaces and molten iron – and the mine pits; still, deep, dark cooling pools, from which would come the hiss of steam when white hot iron was plunged in.

And scattered throughout the Wealden forest there were those charcoal burners' enclosures – the hut and the kiln, the piles of cut limbs and branches, and the solitary, wrinkled charcoal burner.

And when the charcoal burner died, as often as not his body rotted away in solitude and there was no-one to miss him, as the forest retook the enclosure – and the hut and the kiln subsided back into the ground. And there were plenty of charcoal burners scattered throughout the Weald to supply the iron foundries.

Sometimes bits of body were collected – no-one knew by whom. Someone dark. Someone with a book. Someone in those woods. Something. Bits of body were fixed together – bits of this, that and the other. Higgledy piggledy wiggledy. A brain animated by a spark of fire from a bloomer – an ancient blast furnace; a clay chimney – or fluxed into awareness and motion by an organism usually associated with rot and decay – the body jerked into some sort of life.

These composite creatures were known – they were feared of course, because they were emblems of death, pieces of blasphemy, but generally they caused no harm – they were like all of the 'other people' – something you might catch a glimpse of out of the corner of your eye; never to be seen straight on – something to propitiate with a gesture or a morsel of food – something to get away from.

The stories spread; but they drifted away from whispered local legends and took other forms. The Shelley family lived on the edge of the Weald and those stories were passed down to Percy Bysshe Shelley who must have mentioned them to his lover and wife-to-be, Mary. Challenged to produce a horror story, she came up with Frankenstein's monster and as, at the time of the challenge, she was surrounded by Alpine scenery, she set the story in that grand landscape – but at the heart of it there was really a wriggling organism that helped to bring life out of putrefaction in a lost Wealden clearing.

And who was it who constructed that bogus creature at Piltdown? The medieval skull and orang-utan jaw that appealed to the newspapers and the public rather more than it did to palaeontologists. Was it Charles Dawson, who the newspapers called "The Wizard of Sussex"? Was he resentfully looking for acceptance by the academic world from which this non-Oxbridge man, a mere bookseller, felt excluded, by constructing something that would fit the naïve concept of a 'missing link' in a linear chain of human evolution; or was he drawing on old wizardly Sussex stories, piecing together bones, digging in old gravel pits, wondering what eyes were watching him from the woods, as he made his own Piltdown Man?

And the missing link, the stitched-together segments of human and beast, of times and places, of skin, fur, feathers, flesh and stories; could this absorb the resentment of an English antiquarian? Or the wild and suppressed imagination of a woman considered to be an adjunct to a male poet? Or the thoughts of a hundred shunned and inarticulate charcoal burners? Or the gruntings and snufflings and immediacy of the beasts of the forest? A creature that was a piece of Sussex itself – soil and chalk, and the memory of a trillion crustaceans, compressed over aeons to create the rock and soil womb out of which all this was ripped: a geological, caesarean section. And then those hands, someone stumbling through the woods, stitching, snipping, cutting things up, stitching them together. A story.

But it wasn't so long ago that something gained some sort of a consciousness in the Weald. If he was missing, he didn't know what he was missing from, and if he was a link, he had no idea what he could be linking. To call him Link is convenient, but he was no more or less of a link than anything else. Maybe he should be called Crow Man, or Magpie Man, because there seemed to be a lot of corvid in his make-up – but Link will do.

Snuffling with leaves and soil in his nose – fluxed into life by a warmth created by rotting, decomposing organisms – or maybe by lightning, but probably never anything so sharp and sudden, Link lay for three days and three nights. His eyes tried to focus on the tree canopy, he turned his head to the side and coughed mucus into the dead leaves and live soil, then he drifted down into the otherworld, where he felt he belonged, where he could communicate, speak, where time was different.

"You don't belong here", she said, "You're not a bloody fairy, or an elf, or any of the other stuff people make up in their fey moments."

"They make up much more sinister stuff than that", he said, "I could be a troll or an ogre."

"You aren't", she said, and puffed him back up to the surface – and then he couldn't pull himself down to the otherworld again. It was beyond his grasp, his fingers, and he hated that.

Picking himself up, his body full of aches and stings, he leant against a tree, before lurching a few steps forward and falling over. With his mouth open to leaf litter and soil, he wished himself below again, down in the otherworld, but it didn't work – so he lay there, face down, wet, shitty – and with no-one to screech, "I never asked to be born" at. A worm tasted good, though.

Eventually he dragged himself up again, and lurched forwards, shambling on a foot and a folded claw. The road was terrifying – the buzz that he had heard from the woods, became a roar, with the vehicles hurtling along at impossible speeds – and the hard surface of the road hurt his foot and clashed against his claw.

There was a memory, something hazy in his mind. It was a thought of the people who had torn the place apart – of the smoke and flame and hammering – of copper-skinned people and blast furnaces, of people bent double and bandy-legged, of spittle and toothlessness. When he glimpsed people now, from behind trees, or from his frequent position – lying on his belly on the ground – they were hideous looking, all pale like pond creatures, soft and fleshy, smooth. They looked, he thought, like giant larvae; translucent, ready to pupate.

Their litter was everywhere: buildings, enclosed pieces of land, dazzling lights. Always, shining lights and smooth surfaces. His fingers touched plastic and glass, his wing brushed against Perspex, and he recoiled at the cold, unfriendly deathlessness. Things that were close seemed distant – the glass in the UPVC surface of a window frame, a surface of nothingness, was to Link the dead reflection of a distant past, though he knew nothing of its manufacture, of the sand, the product of aeons of water eroding rock, that had been melted into invisibility.

And the cars hurtling past, the roar, the Doppler effect as they moved out of Link's window frame of reference – a brief glimpse of people in another world – close, then gone, shut away; separate.

Sometimes he wondered whether to throw himself under one of those cars – he'd already become familiar with the sight of all the dead creatures on the road – and so end up like the poor old badger, or the fox, or the round, flat hedgehog.

Always hiding from people, recoiling from their pallid faces, he stumbled across fields and hedgerows, crossing roads when he had to, through Cackle Street and Fairwarp, skirting Groaning Bridge and Crowborough, till ahead of him, shining like a vast mythical city from the stories – a mighty metropolis – a place of light and bustle, juggling traffic and people: Tunbridge Wells.

He lurked in shrub beds and the vegetation on roundabouts, and sometimes rested by hanging upside down from lamp posts, swinging, unmolested, next to the lights that hurt his brain. Occasionally someone caught a glimpse of him, but it was never more than a glimpse.

Beast of Tunbridge Wells

The **Beast of Tunbridge Wells** or the **Kentish Apeman** is a cryptid reported by the residents of the county of Kent, England (presumably in and around the town of Royal Tunbridge Wells). The apeman is described as a Bigfoot-like creature that is 8ft tall, with demonic red eyes, long arms and long fingers.

Sightings

Over the past six months there have been a number of sightings of a mysterious beast. Locals in the Kent town have mixed opinions about the claims – with some believing it could be a joker wearing a fancy-dress costume. Sightings in the town go back decades. The Kentish Apeman was first spotted on the town's common during World War II, 70 years ago. A man called 'Graham S' told a story of how an elderly couple saw it in 1942. Writing for the community website *Tunbridge Wells People*, he said: "They were sitting on a bench when they became aware of a 'shuffling noise' behind them."

Fandom

Recoiling from these encounters, he took refuge in the woods on Tunbridge Wells Common, lying on his face, despairing of consciousness. To his relief he found himself sinking down into the otherworld. The sun shone, a soft breeze stirred the tree branches. He looked around for the old woman, but instead he saw a depressed-looking figure sitting on a log. The figure had horns, a pointy tail, cloven hooves, and a bandage on his nose.

"Who are you?" asked Link.

"I'm the devil", said the devil.

"THE devil? The big one? The Great Beast? The fallen angel?"

"Oh, where did you get all this knowledge from?" said the Great Beast, who didn't look very great, and who had a very nasal voice. Link tried to think his way into hazy memories of someone with a book – but he seemed to get blast furnaces again.

"I asked first", he said.

"Any devil thinks they're the big one, it's the way our very necessary narcissism works", replied Beelzebub, with such surprising self-awareness that Link felt he ought to make an honest reply to the devil's question.

"I don't know where my knowledge comes from. I don't know if I really have any. I can't remember", he said.

"You're a mish mash", said the devil, "Is that a crow's wing you have for a right arm?"

Link flapped his one wing.

"Bloody big crow", said the devil.

"Well", he continued, "I'm not surprised your memory's shot..."

Link momentarily saw an image of a cannon firing.

"... but *my* memory is too clear. I suppose I'm really the devil of Tunbridge Wells, but there was a time that I fell from the firmament and wandered around the Weald quite a bit."

Link settled himself, and folded his right wing, though he didn't have a left one, over his left arm, though he didn't have a right one.

"Once upon a time...?", he said in anticipation.

1: The Piltdown Man

"Once upon a time I wandered the Weald; and I liked it. It was a place of smoke and flame and fire. I liked the clanging of tools and the tearing of metal from rock. I liked the lawlessness and profanity. I liked the production of weapons – so that Britons could go bobbing about the waves blowing people's heads off. I liked the way they'd smuggle cannons across the channel, so that the French could blow Britons' heads off (besides each other's) – you know, I'm partial to a bit of mayhem and misery. I liked the way bodies would rot in the woods, with no holy words said for the souls, though I could never find out who it was that crept around and stitched bodies together again. If he made you, he must have been pissed."

"Don't get so personal", said Link. "Get on with the story."

"Well it was before the cannons were invented when Christianity started coming in, but they were making a wondrous array of murderous stuff: pikes and axes and maces and swords and crossbows and flails and halberds and spear heads and battle axes and caltrops. Christians always had a vendetta against devils, and when Bishop Dunstan came all the way east from the church on the hill in poxy Glastonbury, and set himself up in Mayfield, I knew he was going to be trouble. He'd fit in well in the Weald, because he was fond of blacksmithing, but he'd start building those churches with their tolling bells, and he'd do his best to drive me out. Well, he thought women were put into the world to tempt men from righteousness – Adam and Eve and such – all that; you know?"

Link wasn't sure he did know.

"Sexual desire – they always twisted it, but they were never the only ones. Sin and ownership and wicked temptation."

Link, creeping and crawling around Tunbridge Wells, hiding in shrub beds and bushes, had seen how the pink, larvae-like people would maul at each other, would grunt and groan, push each other away, steam up the inside of cars, and always wiping, wiping stuff up. He didn't know what it was all about – but he felt something – and there were more hazy memories that faded away. He was puzzled, he thought it strange and pointless, but he also had the sense of something fundamental. But then, he saw pigeons mate – twitter and dance and flirt – then quick movement, before they'd pace the branches and roof ridges with their backs to each other. With pigeons, however, there was none of that perpetual wiping stuff up.

"Well, Dunstan would stand in those cooling ponds for the blast furnaces, freezing cold, trying to soften his ardour, so I thought that if I could have a bit of fun with his obsessions, I could shame him out of the Weald altogether. So I did a bit of the old shapeshifting, and transformed myself into a woman… and he grabbed me by the nose with his tongs, and, fuelled as much by his own loin twitching misogyny as by any hatred of devils, throws me all the way here, to Tunbridge Wells.

They made money out of me, the smug bastards. I 'imparted to the waters their chalybeate qualities' – sulphur and iron, ferruginous, all red – and Tunbridge became a spa town for all the fat, idle bastards from London, because of the water. Would you like me to relate a complete history of the growth of Royal Tunbridge Wells?"

"No thank you."

"Please yourself. What do you want, anyway?"

"I don't know."

"Come on; there's usually a reason for entering the otherworld."

"I don't know; I just want to know what's going on, really."

"Don't we all. How were you created?"

"I don't know. I just found myself on the forest floor, and that was that."

"One of those Wealden monsters. Maybe you need to find the instruction manual. Who made you? I never could find out who it was creeping around."

"I don't know."

Link reached for some sort of knowledge inside himself, but touched the edge of a void, a blank space – a gap that was terrifying because of its blankness, its lack of any story.

"You really don't know much, do you? You need to ask that bloody old woman. Go on, go and find the old woman. If I were you, I'd bugger off back to Piltdown."

"Piltdown?"

"Yes, where you came from. You're a Piltdown Man if ever I saw one. Those lost imaginations in the Weald made you, and the way that the Weald was torn apart made you. You're as much a part of those old iron foundries as me or Saint Dunstan – but when it all died, and the Weald became nothing but fragments, and bits and pieces, and roads, and I don't know what – you belonged there more than we did. You're as real as any collection of bits and pieces assembled by a liar, any story, any hoax, any bloody monster. You're Piltdown Man – so go to Piltdown – then maybe you can stop saying 'I don't know' all the time."

And Link felt himself drifting upwards. He flapped his one wing, and started to spin in circles, and for a second he had an aerial view of the devil, who was no longer sitting on a log, but on an iron throne, amidst bellows-puffs of flame – and then Link was face down on the ground; dead leaves and the smell of dog shit.

He pulled himself up to his foot and claw, and, emerging from the shrubs, felt the hard, painful surface of a cycle lane. He hobbled back into the bushes just as a lycra-clad cyclist came hurtling down the lane, helmet camera like a third, protruding eye. Link had thought he was inured, by now, to strange sights, but this creature filled him with fear, and he croaked and flapped his wing. The cyclist caught a glimpse of wing, claw, arm, foot, and a face of mutilations – veered off the cycle lane and flew over the handlebars.

Link laughed – a sound like the alarm call of a magpie – and turning his face, snout, half beak, yellow teeth, beady eyes back towards Piltdown, began to walk, the claw dragging him to one side, the foot correcting to the other side, lop sided, a walk that struggled against itself. But Link felt, for the first time, a sense that there was a destination.

2: NAN TUCK'S LANE

Nan Tuck's Lane through Tuck's Wood
Ride Segment: Buxted, East Sussex, United Kingdom

Distance0.8km
Avg Grade 3%
Lowest Elev 43m
Highest Elev 77m
Elev Difference 34m
2,306 Attempts by 1,619 People

Strava: website for athletes

"Which way soever they be dressed and eaten, they stir and cause a filthy loathsome stinking wind within the body, thereby causing the belly to be pained and tormented, and are a meat more fit for swine than men."

The Hampshire botanist, John Goodyer, from *Gerard's Herbal*, 1621, writing about Jerusalem artichokes.

Like a migrating bird, Link had a sense of direction, though he didn't really know what it was. He had stumbled to Tunbridge against it, because he felt he needed to lean against something, as if the resistance would prevent him from falling on his face – but now he felt easier with it behind his back, like a following wind, propelling him forwards. He knew he had to walk with the rising sun behind him, more or less, and the setting sun ahead of him, though he walked mainly at night. The setting sun was the thing – the burning disc that felt like an end to a story.

His destination was Piltdown, but that felt like going back to a mouthful of soil, and he really wanted to by-pass it, to head towards that golden light in the west.

2: Nan Tuck's Lane

Waking up, wet with rain, one evening in a copse, not so far east of Piltdown, and seeing no golden disc in a dark sky, he stumbled through the trees, down a bank and onto Nan Tuck's Lane. He always hated that hard road surface, and rather than cross the road, as he usually did, he climbed back up into the copse.

"Oh there you are", said the old woman.

Having not, as far as he knew, sunk into the otherworld, Link's first instinct was to hide, to fade into the shadows of trees and dusk, as he usually did when people appeared – but it was her.

"Am I in the otherworld?" he asked, and then, finding that he had a voice, concluded that he was.

"Not really", she said, "we're in one of those bits where they bleed together. I'm a ghost."

"Oh."

"The ghost and the monster – dancing together down Nan Tuck's Lane." She laughed.

"I'm not a monster", he said, offended.

"You are what I say you are, and don't get huffy with me. If I'm the ghost of Nan Tuck, you're a monster."

"I'm tired", he said, "I've been to Tunbridge Wells and met the devil."

"Oh dear me, that was two sad souls together. Come with me and get some rest."

He followed her into a circular clearing in the woods, wherein stood a rickety-rackety wooden hut. She pulled open the door, lifting at the same time because the hinges were made of string, and he went inside to see a pot bubbling over a fire, and bottles and jars, all sitting on wooden shelves.

"What have you been eating?" she asked.

"Grubs, worms, roots, berries – and things that people leave in cartons. Chicken nuggets, burger rolls, greenery."

"Greenery? In cartons? Oh yes; they never eat all the salad that goes with a kebab. You'd wonder why they put it there – it only makes the pitta bread go soggy."

Link was lost again, he ate the detritus, he didn't understand the combinations – they were all historical accidents anyway.

"Sit by the fire. Go on, man."

Man? Is that what he was?

He wasn't quite sure of the warmth of the fire. He liked warmth, he'd basked in the warm air from the heating ducts at the back of a sports centre in Tunbridge Wells, but this heat was very immediate – you had to keep adjusting your distance to it. It was like the sun, but you just opened yourself up to the sun – spread wing and arm, foot and claw, and tried to soak it up.

"I've got Jerusalem Artichoke soup. It's excellent for clearing out the system. Every fart is a step nearer to Jerusalem."

"Where is Jerusalem?"

"Oh, it's just a place. People make pilgrimages there. It gives them a focus. It's stories – not always good for the people who live there, though."

"Am I going to Jerusalem?"

"Just your Jerusalem. But I don't know where that is."

Link drank some soup, and felt the warmth spread through his body.

She looked at him in a manner that was both pitying and slightly stern. It made Link feel that he had to ask something of her.

"Once upon a time?"

"Oh, I was a woman who lived in Rotherfield. They said that I poisoned my husband..."

"Did you?"

"Never you mind what I did... it isn't part of the story. The crowd, the Rotherfield mob, they chased me."

"How did they know you killed your husband?"

"Who said I killed my husband?"

"Why did they think you killed your husband?"

"Because he was dead, why do you think?"

Link shut up.

"I ran to the church of Saint Mary the bloody Virgin, in Buxted, to seek sanctuary."

Somehow Link did know what sanctuary meant. He knew what a burger bun was, but this seemed rather more significant.

"The vicar shut the door against me – bastard – so I ran down the lane, for the woods. I disappeared then, they never found me. It was said that I lived in the woods, by the lane; but they could never find where. All they'd find was a circular patch of ground where nothing would ever grow."

"Did you go into the otherworld?"

"Well, that's just one story."

The Jerusalem artichoke soup started to work on Link, and he blasted off a fart.

"That is not decorous", said the old woman. "Turn your arse to the fire when you pass wind, and spare me the bellows."

Link ripped one off into the fire, and it roared up like a Wealden blast furnace.

"Once upon a time...?" he enquired.

"Well, here's the sentimental one. Once upon a time there were two young men, the sons of merchants from Rotherfield, who were in a carriage, trotting towards Buxted for a night's drinking and card playing with friends. They saw a young woman walking down the lane, so they elbowed each other and sniggered; thinking they could have a bit of sport. They climbed out of the carriage and walked behind her; she turned round and looked frightened and they laughed. She walked faster, they walked faster – she clambered over a gate into a field, and they made a great show and a hullabaloo of throwing each other over the gate. They ran to catch up with her, she ran, and they ran faster – shouting at her to stop; stop – it's only a bit of fun.

Well, then there was the rickety-rackety wooden hut and the girl ran inside, pulling the door too behind her. The men pulled the door open and went inside; laughing.

'Hello, my dears,' I said, 'my, but you're a handsome couple of fine young gentlemen and no mistake'. I enjoyed that. They wanted to know where the girl was.

'Oh, you just sit down by the fire my lovely boys, and she'll be here.'

If I say 'sit in front of the fire', you sit in front of the fire, so they did. The fire grew hotter, and their faces were burning – they tried to pull themselves away, but they couldn't. The fire roared up like it did when you blasted a smelly one into it, and their lips started to crack and their faces to blister.

'Fly away my lovely boys', says I, and they found they were able to flee – flee to the nearest pond to push their faces into the green water.

A few days later, back they come, with their blistered faces and a Rotherfield lynch mob; but there was no hut and nothing to show that there had ever been anything there, except the patch of ground where no plant will ever grow."

"Serves them right", said Link.

"Well, of course it does, but if it's not in the otherworld, things generally don't go that way. Here's the other story."

"I didn't say 'Once upon a time'."

"Don't get uppity with me, monster. These are stories, and there are always threes – so you'll listen to the third story whether you like it or not.

Nan Tuck was a girl that lived on the edge of the woods. It was after the civil war; everyone had gone mad. A girl alone, making a little by selling spells and potions, was someone you could lay all your blame and all your guilt on – especially if she didn't have a man. They cried 'witch', and they chased her into the woods and hanged her. Little wonder her ghost should haunt the lane, and that nothing will grow where they murdered her."

Link felt a weight of depression on his head.

"Are you that girl?"

"Oh come on; who are you? We are the stories, the relics, the bits and pieces, flotsam and jetsam from a tide of waffle.

Now, my dear, where do you think you are heading for?"

"I was going to Piltdown, but that was to find you. The devil said I should find my instruction manual. Where should I go?"

"Do you have to do what the devil says?"

"Well, I need something to exist for. You told me about Jerusalem. A focus. Is my instruction manual in Jerusalem?"

"Oh dear, I don't know, but I know who put you together. He spent a lot of time wandering the Weald. I liked him, he was a holy man, but no pompous Saint Dunstan. He always liked a drop of Jerusalem artichoke soup – but he was a bit obsessed. Always sticking things together and referring to his bloody book. Heads, bodies and legs – that's what he was playing.

'Why do you do it?', I'd say. 'Life', he'd say. I left him to it."

"Who is he? What's his book? Where is he?"

"Oh, he's Old Tadig, Tadig Kozh, a Breton. I don't know what the book was. I was always suspicious of books. They get in the way of a good story – when people start staring at those bloody squiggles on paper they forget how to hold knowledge in the swirls and patterns of stories in their heads."

"Where is he?"

"Oh, I don't know. West I suppose. I don't know whether he went back to Brittany. If you go, you'll find out. Now, get your head down. Sleep for a day – and when you wake, I'll be gone."

Link wanted to stay in the hut, he felt safe, but he knew he'd be alone when he woke up.

3: THE DEVIL'S DYKE

Myths regarding the formation of the Devil's Dyke:
Local folklore explains the valley as the work of the devil. The legend holds that the devil was digging a trench to allow the sea to flood the many churches in the Weald of Sussex. The digging disturbed an old woman who lit a candle, or angered a rooster causing it to crow, making the devil believe that the morning was fast approaching. The devil then fled, leaving his trench unfinished. The last shovel of earth he threw over his shoulder fell into the sea, forming the Isle of Wight.

Wikipedia

Steyning
Uncertain. Possibly "dwellers at the stone" or "dwellers at the stony place".

Dictionary of place names, University of Nottingham

When Link awoke, on another fuzzy, damp evening, with no golden setting sun in the west, he was lying face down as usual, but he was in a circular patch of bare earth in a copse. The loss of the old woman, and the hut, and the fire, and the Jerusalem artichoke soup, was like an empty space inside him – like the circle of bare earth beneath him.

He stumbled westwards, and, passing through the back garden of a house, felt a longing for the light pouring out of a window – for some shelter, and someone to tell him a story. He peered through the window and saw a woman with her back to him, staring at the screen of a laptop on a table. There was neatness, and glass, and smooth, hard surfaces, and he lost his longing for shelter – at least, this sort of shelter. It was all too bright, too startling, too sharp edged – too much of a contrast to the old woman's rickety-rackety wooden hut.

3: The Devil's Dyke

The scream, provoked by the sight of Link's face, came from the other side of the world, from New Zealand, from the woman who was the other part of the Skype conversation. When the woman in the room looked round, Link's face was gone from the window.

As Link lurched across fields there was a whole arc of light reflected in the sky ahead of him – the lights of Haywards Heath, Keymer and Hassocks. He felt the pain of the lights and an exhaustion with the people and their flickering screens, and so he headed south-west towards a ridge of hills he'd seen in the distance, whilst peering out from Gipp's Wood in the daytime. The railway line near Plumpton Green was a strange thing and he lay down for a while and listened to a singing in the rails. At Westmeston he headed up the steep slope of Ditchling Beacon, looking for air and space to spread arm and wing, and to allow the wind and the sun, and sometimes the rain, to fill him with life. The lights of Brighton, to the south, were brighter than those lights to the north, but he turned his face westwards, to follow the dark ridge between the illuminated settlements.

It was a relief to be away from roads and cars and buildings. But sometimes, up on those South Downs, he was awoken during the daytime by people – and their voices could be louder and more disturbing than the buzz of sound he'd grown used to. Here, they seemed to shout, and they walked with strange sticks, and they seemed to have a sense of self-righteousness, as if they owned all that surrounded them. They irritated Link more than the fumbling people in parked cars in Tunbridge Wells, or the shouting, screaming crowds of children in a school playground in Chailey, or the shuffling, reversing lorries and shouting men in an industrial estate in Newick.

The following morning Link settled down on the edge of a field, next to a great, dry valley.

"Well, you've been heading west all right", said the devil.

Link tried to hide the pleasure he felt in having company again.

"So have you", he said.

"Oh, I just pop up in a few places where I belong – and this valley is most definitely mine."

"It's big – it has space and air", said Link, "Why is it yours?"

"Well, it's named after me – the Devil's Dyke – and for good reason."

"Once upon a time…?"

"God threw me out of heaven."

"Why?"

"You wouldn't understand – you're too simple."

"I'm not simple."

"Oh, no insult. Let's just say that he's a jealous God."

Link gave up trying to understand; he just wanted the narrative; the comforting rhythm of the story – like walking on foot and claw when the ground was level and soft.

"I fell, I tumbled through the firmament, as they say, till I landed with a crash in Sussex. I lay there for a while, befuddled and feeling really rather traumatised, whilst around me Christianity arrived in Sussex with the last of the Romans. Then, with the coming of the Saxons, Christianity was blown away again. Most of England became Christian, but Sussex remained pagan; it was isolated, cut off by the Weald.

Then along came that bloody Saint Wilfrid, a violent saint if ever there was one. He battered the poor old Jutes, who lived around here at the time, something chronic. Churches started to appear all over the Weald and the tolling of those bloody church bells woke me up. Is there no rest for the wicked? So I shouted, 'That's it, I'll drown the lot of you, I swear to God – him up there – I will. I'll dig a dyke and let in the sea, and if I'm not done by the morning I swear I'll go to hell and stay there.'

Now at that time, Old Nan the wise woman, was living in a rickety-rackety wooden hut on the edge of Rag Bottom Copse."

"Is that the old woman?" asked Link.

"Yes, yes. Well, I grafted away, flinging clods of earth in all directions, and so all those panic-stricken hermits and priestly would-be saints hammered on the old woman's door, imploring her help. She muttered and grumbled and half thought that silencing those bloody bells wouldn't be such a bad idea, but realising that her rickety-rackety wooden hut would be swept away with everything else, she thought she'd better foil my plans – there you are, and I'd never been anything less than friendly towards her. 'Crow, Chanticleer', she said to the cockerel, her familiar.

'Cock a doodle doo', said the cockerel, who never was a very enthusiastic familiar, due to his fear of the pot.

'Bloody crow, or you're in the pot with potatoes, and they haven't even been introduced into Europe yet', she snapped.

'COCK A DOODLE DOO', crowed the cock.

'What's that?' says I, 'this can't be. Tisn't near morning.'

'COCK A DOODLE BLOODY DOO', crowed the cock again.

'NO, NO', I shouted, and dug faster.

Old Nan then lit a candle, held it behind a sieve, and raised it up over Mount Harry.

Of course, I thought it was sunrise, so I turned and ran and ran, westwards, away from the rising sun.

So now the trench I dug is the Devil's Dyke, the clods of earth are Cissbury Hill, Rackham Hill, Mount Caburn and the Isle of Wight, and the churches are still dotted all over the Weald. As for me, I didn't stop running until I came to Bognor – which is as close to hell as anywhere."

"Why?"

"Oh, never mind."

"So the old woman was happy to give you trouble – she got the better of you."

"Oh, come on, it's a story, a story. They make me small – ridiculous – because they can't cope with anything too big – elemental. They turn giants into clowns, dragons into comic beasts, nixies into knuckers. They have to think they control the world, stave off death. It's what they do."

"So can you be a more devilish devil? Can you do the business – can you be more elemental?"

"Ha – well, not exactly me. Keep going west. Ask the people at the stone."

"Who are they?"

"West of here – you'll have to go off the hills, though."

"Will you come with me?"

"You know I can't."

With the devil gone, Link folded his wing around himself and slept. A desolate sleep.

The next night he continued west along the ridge, but when the ridge turned south at Truleigh Hill, Link descended the slope and found himself a place to sleep in the woods by a ruined castle.

To his relief he sank into the otherworld – though he was tired and just wanted to sleep.

The old woman was there, and with her a group of people; men, women and children, all looking like people Link remembered. Not translucent and smooth and pale, but copper-coloured, lined, toothless; the adults bent and bandy legged. Link felt relaxed.

"Are these the people at the stone?" he asked.

The old woman grinned.

"You've been dancing with the devil again", she said.

"Just talking", said Link, "I can't dance."

"Oh, just a phrase, just a phrase."

An old man with beady eyes sat next to the old woman and regarded Link closely. Link felt uncomfortable. He felt he had to say something.

"Can you tell me how to find my instruction manual?"

The old man grinned.

"That old saint was always on about devil", he said.

"Old saint? Story?"

The old man spat again. "Story? You ask she."

"You and stories", she said. The people at the stone huddled closer around the fire.

"The dragon ships – they was coming ashore all down the coast. Murdering bastards – like the Saxons before them. Same again and again and again. Well, in Chidham there lived a lad called Cuthman. Chidham's west of here, down near Bosham – you've not got that far yet. Cuthman's old father had been a merchant, trading out of Bosham, and when those bastard Vikings were spotted sailing around Selsey Bill, it was just too much for Cuthman's father to leave his goods to these barbarians and flee to the hills with the rest of the townspeople. So he stayed and tried to protect his goods, and the Vikings did him in. Cuthman, up in the hills, was left alone to look after his mum.

The Vikings had taken everything from the town, including the largest church bell, and when they sailed out of the creek a storm whipped up and the church bell crashed through the side of the long ship and sank the boat. A whirlpool swirled around the sound of the tolling of the sinking bell, and all the other bastards were sucked into the maelstrom and drowned. They took most of the riches of Chidham and Bosham with them, so Cuthman and his old mum were left with nothing, and Cuthman eked out a living as a shepherd, and with little to help him look after his mother.

But Cuthman was one of them Godly types, and he reckoned that the solitary life of a shepherd helped him talk to God. He would draw a pretend circle in the ground and his little flock of sheep would stay in the circle. Cuthman would then kneel upon a stone – he called it the kneeling stone and it's still there near Chidham, and he would pray to God. God spoke to Cuthman.

'Travel north and east', says God, 'till you come to the dark forest wherein dwelt my disciple, Leonard.' Leonard was another of them grumpy old saints. 'Continue the work of Leonard and build a church; for within that dark and unwholesome place, many of the populace are still heathen Wildishers, and you must bring the word of God to them.'

Now, many a saint would have left everyone and everything to do this, for they thought holiness was more important than taking responsibilities – but Cuthman was a practical young man, and he saw the word of God in more than voices heard during contemplation; and being a humane sort of fellow he knew he could never abandon his old mum.

So he upped and built a wheelbarrow, and the barrow had a rope halter which he put around his neck as he trudged through the Sussex mud and up to the high, chalk downs, with his old mother sat in the barrow.

Days later, he looked down at the great Wealden forest and saw a plume of smoke rising up above the tiny village of Warminglid. He trudged along Spronkett's Lane, his old mum bouncing along in the barrow in front of him, and into Earwig Lane. Finally the rope halter could take no more – it snapped, dumping Cuthman's mum into the Sussex mud. There were some peasants in a nearby field, and they all started to laugh.

'Funny!' shouted Cuthman, 'you buggers need to get your sense of humour looked at'. Cuthman's poor old mum just grumbled; 'Bloody mud, bloody missions, bloody wheelbarrow.'

Cuthman then made a new halter out of elder branches – and this made the peasants laugh even more.

'Lummox, nodbucket, spronkett noggin, selig, madbrain mawkin,' they jeered, waving their scythes at him.

'Men mock and heaven shall weep' cursed Cuthman, and the heavens opened; but only over that field, ruining the crop.

Cuthman's mum, though, well, she shouted, 'I'm not going any further into this stinking forest – turn about, son, and head back south if you know what's good for you.'

'Mother,' quoth the Saint, 'the Almighty has instructed me.'

'I'm as almighty as you'll bloody find', says she. 'Turn around, or I'll fetch you one round the ear 'ole.'

Cuthman was a wise saint, and since God didn't seem to be saying anything directly, he reckoned that God was speaking through his mum; so he turned round and headed south again.

It wasn't till he came to the place of the people at the stone that the elder halter broke, once again pitching Cuthman's mother onto her backside.

'I'm not going any bloody further' says she – and so they didn't. Cuthman converted the locals into Christians, and they all built a church, used the old stone as a footstep at the church door, and called the place Steyning.

To this day, though, in the Weald, next to Earwig Lane, there are often strange downpours of rain. Then the earwigs will crawl out from the mossy banks and get inside your shirt and your underclothes. But then, that wouldn't bother you, would it?"

And she was right. It would never bother Link.

"He never went up Chanklebury, though, none of them went up there."

"Chanklebury?"

"Up there. Chanklebury. Chanctonbury Ring."

Link had already noticed that strange crook on the line of hills, the one that always presented itself as a focus.

"The only holy man who would ever dare do that would be Tadig Kozh; but they never made him into a saint. Don't suppose he'd like it if they did."

Link had a sudden rush of hope.

"Will Tadig Kozh be on Chanklebury?"

"I don't know, dear…" she used the word 'dear' with sympathy – Link liked the idea that someone should consider him worthy of sympathy "…he was a Breton, but I don't know where he is now. He may be there, but I don't see why. I think he'll be on a hill, and if I knew I'd tell you. I don't like Chanklebury, though, it's not a good place."

"I need to look."

"I suppose you do, dear."

She puffed Link up to the surface, the woods around Bramber Castle – as he knew she would – but now he felt he had a focus, a destination: Chanklebury. His walk had a purpose.

4: CHANKLEBURY

Circumambulation: (from Latin *circum* around + *ambulātus* to walk) is the act of moving around a sacred object or idol.

Wikipedia

Widdershins: in a direction contrary to the sun's course, considered as unlucky; anticlockwise. "she danced widdershins around him"

English Oxford Living Dictionaries

If you circle Chanctonbury Ring widdershins, at night, and depending on which story you listen to that could be one – three – seven times (there are other combinations in different stories; you may have to go naked, or walk backwards, or only do it under a full moon, or count the trees as you go), then the devil will appear and give you a bowl of soup. When this story is recounted in guide books the writer can seldom resist the temptation to point out that it seems an awful lot of work for a bowl of soup, but who knows what the soup might signify – what was given to someone who circumambulated the hill in the Neolithic? Or the Bronze Age? Or the Iron Age, when the hill fort was constructed? Or during the time when the Romans had a temple there? What offerings were made, what sacrifices, what horrors – or what pleasant hospitalities?

***Sussex Folktales*, Michael O'Leary**

In Steyning, Link felt strangely curious about people, and lurked in the public toilets in the car park, and down a lane by some rather bijou craft shops. He was spotted a couple of times, just as a disappearing shadow, and did cause some alarm – there had already been quite a few sightings of him in Sussex, which had made some of the local papers, and had appeared in a blog written by a young man from Worthing, who was obsessed with both aliens and the supernatural. There was no mention of him in the national press – there was far too much going on in the world for silly season stuff and nonsense, and the reality of politics was stretching credulity enough anyway.

Link did some moving around in the day time – back garden hopping – though he spent a lot of the day sleeping in a garden shed, amidst tins of nuts and bolts, an ancient rusty mower, and a much more modern electric strimmer. He shared the shed with a colony of mice, who lived in a sack of grass seed.

In his garden hoppings, however, he found himself continually looking up and seeing Chanklebury – and at night, looking through the window of the Steyning Bookshop, he saw a picture of it on the front cover of a book, and in the picture it had a much more extensive cover of beech trees. The great storm of 1987 was not something Link knew anything about, but he was a lot closer to that elemental, howling wind than the people who had fearfully lain in their beds as it felled the trees, presenting them in the morning with the shock of a changed Chanklebury.

Link was strangely nervous, as if he was preparing for something, and spent three days and three nights lurking around Steyning, eating grass seed, worms, beetles, some waste vegetables from the back of a shop, and some past-their-sell-by-date defrosted curries from round the back of a mini-mart.

The next night he headed for the hill – past the naked roots of trees, making a lattice wall next to a steep, earthen slope – through the woods – up to the windblown down – for isn't a down always up? Link gazed at the circle of trees and thicket – Chanctonbury Ring – and heard the screech of an owl. It repeated as it circled the copse. Then there was the high-pitched mew of a buzzard. Link was familiar with these sounds – a buzzard was to be heard in the day time, not the middle of the night. The screech, the mew, the high-pitched avian screams, sounding like a human scream that had lost all sense of reason, a thin sound from beyond the narrative of a life, from outside sense and comprehension, circled the copse in opposite directions – meeting and parting, converging and splitting – one clockwise, one anti-clockwise: widdershins.

Link headed towards the copse, but then felt the imbalance of foot and claw take him sideways, around it. He leaned against his sense of direction, his migrating instinct, and staggered eastwards, but then, following the perimeter of the copse, he found himself propelled westwards, like a bicycle freewheeling down a hill; but then eastwards again, into first gear, pushing against the force of a strange gravity.

Three times, widdershins, Link circled the copse – then he limped into the trees, searching for the devil.

As he expected, he sank into the otherworld. He looked for the devil, and a story – but all he felt was darkness, and a great weight upon his head and shoulder – heavy, like fathoms of ocean – crushing him. Then a faint light, and there was the face of the devil. Link couldn't say "Once upon a time…", he opened his mouth, his not quite a beak, and heard a distant groan. The devil looked at him beseechingly, with a "help me" in his eyes, as something pushed him down beneath Link. Link held out his hand, trying to catch the devil's hand and pull him back up, but Beezlebub, squashed, crushed, was pushed further down into darkness.

A child with a shifting face proffered a bowl of soup. Link couldn't keep up with the changing features and expressions of the child, but he felt that there must be comfort from the soup – he longed for the old woman's Jerusalem artichoke soup; warmth and company and stories and the relieving release of farts blasting into the fire. But the soup looked gelatinous, like congealing blood, and then its sticky viscosity took on the appearance of all those bodily emissions the people of Tunbridge Wells were endlessly wiping up. Link was used to eating worms and woodlice, cold and old sweet and sour chicken; even vomit – the projectile waste of drunken evenings. But this soup disgusted him. He heard the screams of sacrifice, the desolation of despair, a bleakness beyond anything he'd yet experienced in a lonely wander through the broken landscape of the hopeless larva people. The words, "I don't want your filthy soup" formed in his head – and he pushed it away with a wing, feeling that he was pushing through gloop, through heavy liquid. He tried to swim, climb, force his way upwards, and found himself caught in a tangle of beech tree roots – and there was the face of a man, twisted into the roots, struggling to escape, but with every tug, every turn, trapping him further. The man looked at Link with the same beseeching expression that the devil had shown, and Link tried to reach him, as he'd tried to reach the devil, but all there was were twisting roots, and Link being dragged downwards again, and a weight of depression, like the sack of grass seed with the mice wriggling in it, crushing his head.

He tried to call to the old woman, but she wasn't there, and then he felt the words "Tadig Kozh" and caught hold of a hand.

"I didn't ask to be born" was in Link's head, "Who do you think you are?"

The hand, strong arm, pulled Link up and through the roots, and he lay alone, face down in the centre of the copse before hearing the screech again. He hauled himself upright, and, in as much as he was capable of running, he ran, ran westwards, his migratory instinct thankfully behind his back, pushing him west. His usual instinct for hiding was gone as he put as much distance between himself and Chanklebury as he could.

One person saw him and froze with horror. One person camping out near Chanctonbury Ring for their own obscure purposes. But then, they were flirting with horror, and that's what they thought they'd got. It was only Link, though, just Link travelling west, running away, running towards – with a migratory instinct at his back and the line of the South Downs ahead of him.

5: AMBERLEY WILD BROOKS

"He was called 'Lord Moon' and remembered for his feats of running over the river, and catching hold of the sweeps of windmills while revolving, and going around with the vanes. Once in a high wind at Amberley Mill he was thrown over a 16ft high fence, but falling on newly ploughed land, it broke his fall without serious injury. Another amusement of his was running on top of quickset hedges with youths on terra firma, and beating them."

Rev. E. Noel Staines, in *Dear Amberley*, quoting the local paper of 1854

"Amberley Wild Brooks – what a delicious name! – all flooded into a great sheet of water in wet winters, add further mysteries and charms to the place in the artist's eye. But the villagers, not unnaturally, perceive certain disadvantages in all this soaking water – though the village itself stands high enough out of it. The classic Amberley story is that when the local inhabitant is asked in the summer where he lives he answers proudly 'Amberley, where would you?' But the same question in winter brings forth the mournful response, 'Amberley, God knows!'. Other Sussex villagers have been known to declare that the dwellers in Amberley grow web-footed."

Esther Meynell, *Sussex*, 1947

Link hurried, stumbled, along the ridge, till he came to a gap, carved by the River Arun, scouring its way through to the sea. He tumbled downhill, through Rackham Banks, and into a flat, wet, amphibious sort of a land: Amberley Wild Brooks. He was away from people and houses, roads and cars, and after Chanklebury he felt relieved to be on low-lying land.

It was wet, bubbling, gloopy. Mud and chalk and water. The sudden splash of a fish, and the twirl of a mini-whirlpool by an outlet pipe. Link sat by the bank of a drainage ditch and put himself into another world of scale, where the whirlpool was a maelstrom, and pond skaters where huge, aquatic dinosaurs. He regarded the reflection of the full moon, hoping the light would lift some of the Chanklebury darkness away from him.

"Ugly monster", said the moon-faced figure sitting next to him.

Link, realising he'd drifted into the otherworld, and fearful of the suffocating darkness he'd escaped from, continued to gaze at the moon's reflection.

"On Amberley Swamp, it's always damp", said the irritating voice, made even more irritating by "rhyming" swamp and damp.

"Fuck off", said Link, picturesquely.

"Oooh; it's a sweary monster – now you can communicate."

Link looked at the round headed, marionette-like figure sitting next to him.

"Who are you?"

"Lord Moon. I can dance better than you.

There was an old woman tossed up in a basket,
Tossed high in the sky by Lord Amberley Moon.
What she did there, I couldn't but ask it,
For in her hand she carried a broom.
"Old woman, old woman, old woman", says I,
"Oh where are you going, up so high?"
"To sweep the cobwebs from the sky,
And dance with a knucker, and eat Churdle Pie."

"There was an old woman – is she here?" Link wanted to see her – he wanted to express his anger. Why did she let him go to Chanklebury? Really, though, he longed for the warmth and security of the rickety-rackety wooden hut.

"The monster, the monster,
Lived under the hill.
And if he's not gone,
He lives there still."

5: AMBERLEY WILD BROOKS

Lord Moon leaped across the drainage ditch, capered down the other side, then jumped back.

"Follow me, thing. She's here."

Link followed reluctantly as Lord Moon pranced from side to side, and occasionally turned somersaults, and there, next to a copse of willows, at a conjunction of ditches, was the rickety-rackety wooden hut.

"Ugly badger, crow man,
Come to see you, Old Nan."

The door creaked open, and she regarded Link solemnly.

"Oh my, you've made it. Come on inside."

She looked at Lord Moon as he flitted about.

"Go on, you've got mischief to be making. Go and scare some night fishermen or some such."

Once inside, Link dropped onto a chair that was as rickety-rackety as the hut.

"Why did you send me there?" he asked, wearily.

"I didn't – you chose it. I didn't know how it was going to be. Not good, I see, it could have been right. No Tadig Kozh, then?"

"I think he pulled me out, I think it was his arm."

"Ah, then you'd have done most of the work yourself."

"Don't I always?"

"Yes, yes, you do, you do. Listen now – stay awhile. This isn't a bad place."

"I thought I didn't belong in the otherworld; 'You're not a bloody fairy, or an elf, or any of the other stuff people make up in their fey moments'", said Link bitterly.

"Oh, all right. No; you're more real than that." She spoke sharply, but there was something that might have been a touch of respect in her voice.

"Now sit down, and we'll have some Jerusalem artichoke soup. And mind your manners."

So Link stayed in Amberley Wild Brooks, unclear much of the time if he was in the otherworld or not. The winter came; not a particularly cold or frozen winter – but out in the damp of the levels, the wild brooks, it was always cold; except next to the old woman's fire.

Link liked it there. The old woman had a companion magpie, which liked to sit on Link's shoulder, and make its harsh, jabbering cry; and Link felt that it was company. Lord Moon was company too, but irritating – constantly flicking things at Link, and calling him names. It was pleasing to watch him flicker over the swamp, though, a light fading, reappearing, jumping the ditches and twisting through the willows, disappearing to the furthest reaches of the swamp, towards the steeple of Bury Church, and then hurtling back again, spinning past Link's outstretched wing, and ruffling his feathers.

When spring started to make itself known, the willows started to bud, and the old woman took the tables and chairs outside and started to sweep the earthen floor with a besom, announcing that she was spring cleaning, Link knew that it was time to leave.

"And where do you think you're going?" she asked, in her rather peremptory manner.

"It's a hill – he's on a hill, but it wasn't Chanklebury."

"...and you're sure it's a hill",

"No."

"Well, that's helpful, dear."

"The devil once told me about Saint Dunstan, he'd come from Glastonbury. Is that a hill? Is that where a holy man would live?"

"Oh, that's for sure. Glastonbury Tor, yes. Everything's holy there. A hill with a church tower on it, and stories."

Link felt a surge of hope.

Is it west of us?"

"It certainly is, but there's a lot between here and there."

"Will Tadig Kozh be in Glastonbury?"

"You really think that, after all this time, I wouldn't tell you if I knew? Tadig Kozh was Breton, but he may be anywhere, on any hill. Glastonbury is so full of saints and holy people, and old kings and queens, and pilgrims, and charlatans, and seekers, and priests, and the whole run of crashing bores – he may have gone there to join them; though in my memory he was always a more solitary fellow. There's a big Tesco, there, though; always plenty of waste food."

Link felt that he had no option but to trust his sense of direction. Up on Chanklebury, when he thought he'd reached his destination, it still pulled him westwards. He should have continued to follow it.

For the first time Link had to say goodbye. He wasn't being puffed out of the otherworld to find himself alone again; he had to physically tear himself away from a place where he felt comfortable – to deliberately make himself alone again.

He left the hut in the early evening. The old woman didn't prolong the agony by waiting at the door – she went back inside, hauling the door shut behind her. The magpie screeched and chattered, and flew its juddering flight above Link, as he headed for Amberley Castle.

Lord Moon skimmed across a drainage ditch and somersaulted over Link.

"Bye, Baby Bunting
Daddy's gone a'hunting.
Gone to get a story skin,
To wrap his silly feelings in."

"Fuck off", said Link.

Lord Moon sniggered and bounced along beside Link like a luminous space hopper.

"I could make you fit their world – and I could make you look like one of them."

"Who? People?"

"Yes, yes – you could talk like you can now – you could be with them. No hiding."

Link paused. Was this so? Lord Moon was so untrustworthy – and Link didn't know if he wanted to look like one of the larva people. But – to be one of them, to take a part, to shake off this monstrous loneliness.

5: AMBERLEY WILD BROOKS

They passed a pond at the foot of Amberley Castle; a castle that wasn't a castle but looked like one. The wall had holes for nesting doves, but there were also jackdaws, and the two types of bird seemed to be competing for dominance. The magpie gave its chattering cry and turned back into the wild brooks.

Lord Moon and Link came to a road.

"Well?" said Lord Moon.

"Go on, then", said Link.

Lord Moon screeched with laughter and bounded away over the swamp.

Link looked down at his two feet, and his pink trainers. He walked down the side of the road – female, teenage. He/she was picked out in the headlights of a car – and felt no need to hide. The car passed on along the road, and up a hill. Link listened to the sound of its engine fading away into the distance. She walked on. Different body, different feelings, different way of walking – but still Link. Another car passed, and then stopped. Link drew level, and the window smoothly opened.

"Where are you going?" said the young man.

"Littlehampton" said Link.

She had no idea why she said "Littlehampton" – it was just there in her story – she was from Littlehampton. Sometimes, on the wild brooks, Link had watched the night fishermen by the river at Bury and heard them talk. They often came from Littlehampton, if they didn't come from Worthing.

"You should come with us", said the young man, "we're going to a party in Arundel."

Link was immersed enough in the young woman's story to feel a difference between the way she talked and the way the young man talked. The young man was amused and his voice also contained a level of excitement and contempt.

"Are you going west?" asked Link.

The question made the young man laugh.

"Are you going west?" he imitated, in an accent not his own; "to San Francisco?"

The driver laughed.

"Get in", said the young man, "we'll go to the party. You'll be able to drink something better than WKD, or Kopparberg." The driver laughed again.

Link didn't answer and climbed into the back seat. The car continued up the hill, past the George and Dragon at Houghton, whilst the young man in the front passenger seat, with a great deal of laughing and wriggling, climbed over his seat, and tumbled into the back next to Link. Link saw a vivid picture of two young men tumbling over a gate in a story, and a young woman running to a rickety-rackety wooden hut. She felt the atmosphere in the car tighten, constrict, become claustrophobic, like being inside Chanklebury. The space belonged to the two young men – the one putting his arm around her in the back seat, the other with his eyes flickering between the road and the rear-view mirror – watching, grinning.

"What's your name?" said the young man.

"Sky", said Link. Sky? Both young men laughed.

"I suppose you only talk to Annabelles", said Link. Where did that name come from? What was all this shit in her head? An echo of Lord Moon's laughter danced around the inside of her skull.

"That's a nice tattoo" the young man breathed into her ear, looking at the tattoo of flowers on her wrist, "I bet you've got one on your back."

"No", she said, "no". She was Link. Monster. Now she was afraid – stuck in a place that seemed to be shrinking and compressing the air inside the space. Big, blue eyes.

"Oh, what big eyes you have, my dear"

The driver laughed; "All the better to see you with."

Link wished she had her wing back, her claw, her smell, her badger, crow, wild boar, charcoal burner remains. The pupils of her eyes started to blacken and shrink.

"What a big mouth you have, my dear." The driver sniggered.

The young man's hands were moving down her neck to her breasts.

"What big ..."

A wing encircled the young man, there was a face of scars and stitches, there was fur and feathers – a wriggling of insects. The young man forgot to scream as the wing started to squeeze and snap his ribs – his eyes were bigger as they protruded from his face. The driver remembered to scream, as he looked in the mirror, and the car hit the Whiteways roundabout, before bouncing into a tree, turning over and coming to rest upside down.

Link crawled out and felt the hot stickiness of his own blood. He staggered more than usual. His physical pain mixed with his own memories, the strange, incomprehensible memories of a young woman from Littlehampton, and ancient memories of the Weald; of blast furnaces and a charcoal kiln; all away in the deep, dark woods.

He limped through the woods towards the River Arun – briefly eastwards, leaning on his sense of direction for support. He'd walk northwards along the river bank; it would take him back to the Amberley Wild Brooks, back to the old woman and the rickety-rackety wooden hut. He wanted her healing, her Jerusalem artichoke soup – and he wanted to strangle Lord Moon, to extinguish his lights, to take out his bounce, to squash his face into Amberley Swamp. But Link knew the old woman wouldn't be there. There would be no easy access to the otherworld. He looked at the full moon in the sky, raised his head, and tried to howl like a wolf. But what came out was the squeal of a wild boar. He felt his stitches unravelling, snapping, scars opening, and, holding his own neck, turned southwards, following the river through the southern reaches of the Levels, and on, through Arundel. In the distance he could hear sirens.

6: KNUCKERHOLE

Deep and "fathomless" pools were also a source of dragon legend. There is one at Lyminster, near Arundel, called the Knucker Hole (or Nuck Hole, there are variants in spelling) which never freezes in the most severe winters and was in early days reputed to be the haunt of a dragon, whose fiery breath would naturally keep any foes at bay. This dragon used to prey upon the unfortunate inhabitants of those regions, as well as upon their cattle, carrying the victims off to the swampy regions of the Arun to consume them.

Esther Meynell, *Sussex*, 1947

Binsted Farmer Luke Wishart writes that the 'Knacker Hole' in Burgess's Field, south of Goose Green, "was a mythical hole, like the one at Lyminster which houses a dragon. Said to be the home of dragons, and bottomless". His father Ernest Wishart had looked into this in the 1920s: there was talk of 'water witches'. Luke however being of a scientific frame of mind, "arranged to place our irrigation pump into it to test the water capacity. The pump ran dry in just over 10 hours, and we could see the bottom. It filled up rapidly as soon as we stopped pumping. We didn't find any dragons – but ... they may have escaped overnight."

Mike Tristram. http://www.binsted.org/folklore

In the early hours of the morning there was still traffic on the A27 dual carriageway. As the road headed westwards it did a strange thing – simply came to a stop, forcing traffic onto a slip road, which led onto a single carriage way around Arundel. It was as if the road was avoiding something.

Link skirted the road junction, where the slip roads headed down, one towards Littlehampton, and the other round the edge of Arundel, and found himself crossing a service station and lorry park. He found some scraps to eat round the back of a McDonald's, climbed a fence into the flat, marshy fields behind, and lay down – hurting, unable to fold his wing properly, feeling component parts of his body tearing apart. In his face a segment of wild boar was disattaching from something that used to be part of a medieval charcoal burner.

The devil was sitting on a stone.

"Do you know where this stone came from?" asked the devil.

"I don't care", said Link, "I'm hurting."

"The giant Bevis threw it – he was guarding the gates of Arundel Castle, and he threw it at a dragon."

"I don't want any stories; I hurt."

"I've not been feeling that great myself", answered the devil, "I don't suppose you'd like to enquire after my well-being?"

Link had a vision of the devil being dragged down into Chanklebury.

"Sorry", he said, "I tried to help you."

"Yes, you did – but there's not much help anyone can give against that suffocating darkness."

Link thought about the horror of it all, and of how there seemed to be no surviving it.

"How did you get out?"

"I was dragged down into the hill; I hoped I'd get to the flames of hell and my iron throne – but there was just a void, a horrible nothing, no existence, no story; nothing. I cried that I wanted hell; hell or Sussex; I wanted some reality but, please, not this blankness. Well, hell was there somewhere, because a flame entered the void and touched water from the hill, from the chalk. Would you like me to tell you about the drainage system and catchment area of the South Downs? It's very interesting."

"No, thank you."

"Oh well, but out of the flame and the water came steam, and out of steam came a knucker."

Link was too hurt and weary to enquire what a knucker was; he let the devil carry on talking.

"She – he – not sure – was part of the void itself. She was made of nothing, of a chaos of disorder, blank spaces, no words, no thoughts. Not hell, not heaven; emptiness. We drifted into a tunnel, and I gave myself up to all that rolling and floundering and bubble-blowing – water – greenness. She took me to a knuckerhole. It's just down the way from here. A few fields away at Lyminster. We're in knuckeridoodle land. No road should ever cross this."

Link, his body seemingly collapsing and splitting apart, didn't ask any questions. The devil gave him a sympathetic look, and said, "Let's get you fixed up. I'll do some stitching; and then we'll get you to the knuckerhole; there's healing in there. We'll hide in that copse of trees, so we're not disturbed when all the bloody people wake up."

The sun wasn't visible as it rose; there was a dull light from behind clouds and Arundel, with its castle and cathedral, seemed to slowly materialise, looking out from the high ground, out over the flat land between the Downs and the sea.

As the devil cut and stitched, pushing stitches made from ligaments back into place, stretching and tying, he coaxed Link's car crash story from him.

"That's an old story", said the devil, "but you gave it a most satisfactory end."

"The old woman told me three stories about Nan Tuck's Lane – but she said that if the stories aren't in the otherworld, they don't generally go the way you want them to. I just wanted a bit of justice."

"Well, it didn't end up too great for you; you're in a mess. Still, best of three I suppose."

"Do you remember telling me a story about Saint Dunstan?" asked Link.

"Oh, that twat. Yes, of course."

"You said he came from Glastonbury, a church on a hill. I think Tadig Kozh lives in or around a hill. Do you think he's in Glastonbury?"

"Tadig Kozh?"

6: KNUCKERHOLE

"The old woman says he's the one who made me."

"Does she now. Well, you'll have to ask her."

"I have, she doesn't know."

"Well, don't expect me to know; I'm only Beelzebub, what do I know about anything?"

There was a distant rattling; the sound of a train. "Listen", said the devil, noticeably changing the subject, "ticketty tock, ticketty tock. Don't you love a train?"

Link was bewildered.

The devil went all glassy-eyed and blissful; "Pulborough, Amberley, Arundel, Littlehampton", he intoned, "Clymping, Barnham, Bognor. Ticketty tock, ticketty tock."

Link gave up on the conversation.

After the devil had completed what seemed an age of pinching and stitching, they rested in the copse until the sun sank into the flat knuckeridoodle land to the west, the lights of Arundel on the hill turned into stars, and the castle and cathedral faded into the darkness.

They headed south through fields, fences and hedgerows. Link always hated barbed wire – brambles and thorns never presented him with any difficulty, however dense and entwined – but barbed wire could pull out stitches, and tear at feathers, skin and fur. The devil was able to just touch barbed wire with a finger nail, so that it sprang, dangerously, apart. Link liked that.

They reached a chain link fence around a pond. Scaling it was easy for Link.

"Knuckerhole", said the devil. "This is knuckeridoodle land."

"There is something different about it", said Link.

"All this flat land – well, flattish – down to the sea, down to bloody Bognor. There used to be a lot of knuckerholes – good water that keeps its temperature. Go and see the knucker, she'll help you."

The surface of the water started to bubble and boil, and a large dragon's head popped out. It shook itself, like a dog after a swim, and looked at the devil.

"How do, devil?" said the knucker.

"How do, knucker?" said the devil.
"I'm not a she, I'm a he."
"So you are", said the devil.
The knucker looked at Link.
"How do, monster?" said the knucker.
"How do, knucker?" said Link, trying not to be offended.
The knucker looked at the devil.
"What you doing back? Did you bring me a churdle pie?"

Churdle

Pastries – Sweet Double Crust Pies

Sussex

A type of pasty made by piling a circle of paste with a chopped mixture of cooked liver, bacon, and herbs (sometimes with apple or mushrooms) topped with cheese and breadcrumbs. The edges pulled up and pinched together in the centre, egg-washed and baked.
The origin of the name is obscure, it may be connected with the old usage of 'churd' to mean 'to turn over' (as in 'churn' or 'churned'). There are recent references to the dish being 17th century and possibly that it is associated with Chichester, but we can't find any definitive sources.

The Foods of England Project:
www.foodsofengland.co.uk/churdle

"Oh, you don't get any decent pies any more – this is Sussex – it's all sun-dried tomatoes and fettu-fucking-cine nowadays."

Link thought about the scraps he'd picked up from behind the McDonald's, and the devil, sensing his thoughts, said, "Whatever – we don't talk about that."

6: KNUCKERHOLE

The knucker sniffed Link, as if wondering whether to eat him or not. Then, looking at the devil, he blew a bubble, which popped, leaving a puff of smoke.

"Nick, Knock, Knacker,
Give the dog a bone.
Old Nick and the Knucker,
Come rolling home."

"Very nice", said the devil, "Go on, tell my monster friend the story. The droll."

"Taint that much of a story", said the knucker, "usual stuff. I was terrorising the neighbourhood, eating cattle and folk and all, and then I was going to eat a princess, from up Arndle way. Anyhow, a knight come along and slew me and married the princess, and that was that."

"That's a shit story", said the devil. "Give us another."

"This time there weren't no knight. There was Jim Pulk. He fed me a churdle pie; it were too dense and I got the collywobbles. Well, seeing as Rennie's hadn't been invented, I was writhing around a bit, and Jim upped with a felling axe, and lopped off my head."

The devil gave a sharp intake of breath. "Ooooh, nasty. Go on – there's always three – tell him the other."

"Well, Jim Pulk bet Jim Puttock that the knuckerhole wasn't bottomless, so they got one of the bells from Saint Mary Magdalene church, down over there, and lowered it down, but it never touched the bottom. Then the rope slipped between their hands, and down went the bell – bong, bong, bong – and bounced off my knuckernut. Well, the silly buggers went and got another bell, and didn't they go and lose that one too. And then another; same thing. Ever since then the church has only got six bells. You see eight is best: do ray me fa so la ti do."

"The diatonic scale" said the devil knowledgably, "plus one."

"...and the pub is called the Six Bells 'n all" added the knucker.

"Well", he continued, "them bells bouncing off me nut woke me up, so up I come, and back to the old terrorising and that. Jim Pulk baked a giant churdle pie and put a load of poisonous mushrooms and deadly nightshade berries in it. He hoisted it up on a cart wot was pulled by six white oxen."

"Yes, of course, always six white oxen" said the devil, who was starting to be a bit irritating with his knowledgeability.

"Anyhows, I ups and ate the pie, the dish, the cart, and the six white oxen. I gets poisoned, I keels over stone dead, and Jim Pulk offs with my head. Off he goes down to the Six Bells, drinks a celebratory pint and wipes his mouth. Well after mashing up them shrooms and the berries, he'd never washed his hands, so he poisons himself and drops down dead 'n all. His gravestone, the Slayer's Stone, is over there in the church."

"Well, I'm glad to see that you're not dead", said Link courteously.

The devil looked at Link.

"You see; it's me and the Devil's Dyke, me and Saint Dunstan. All turned to a little story, a droll. But there's more to it than that. Do you know the Nixie? The Nycor?"

"Not personally."

"Ha ha. She's Jenny Greenteeth. She's Peg Powler. She's Grindylows. She's the blank eyed monster of the pond. She's Grendel's mother."

"Grendel's mother?"

"Beowulf. Get educated. Ask that bloody Tadig Kozh. Grendel's mother could take to you I dare say, all rag a ma tag – you'd remind her of poor Grendel. You've both done in a few annoying blokes. Anyhow, a knucker is pretty much a nixie, if the stories will allow. Dive into the pond and go with the dragon."

"Are you coming?"

"No, I think I'll go to Bognor Regis, I'll be comfortable there; plenty of work for a devil. Go on, catch hold of the dragon's tail."

The dragon submerged his head into the water with a hiss of steam and stuck his pointy tail into the air.

6: KNUCKERHOLE

"Go on, go on", shouted the devil. "Have a good journey my old mate."

Link clutched the dragon's tail, and found himself being plunged down into the green, green water of the Lyminster Knuckerhole.

At first it was helter-skelter, and hanging on for dear life with hand and claw, hurtling downwards, spiralling – holding his breath – until, forced to breath in, he found that he could, and the mad plunge downwards faded into a gentle drift, and the dragon wasn't a dragon, but a woman, green and sinuous, not a woman, a serpent, then a serpent-woman, and then there was a soft voice in his ear:

"Rock a bye baby,
On the tree top.
When the winds blow,
The cradle will rock.
When the bough breaks,
The cradle will fall,
Down will come baby,
Cradle and all.

Rock a bye baby,
Thy cradle is green.
Ugliest baby,
That ever was seen.
But beastie is real,
Beast's got a soul.
He's about to be born,
Out of my hole."

Link drifted passively through the fluid, he felt the hot pain, where the devil had re-stitched his scars, fade away, and the aching inside his body began to fade and diminish.

The Nixie put her arms around him.

"Go on, find the silly man. Tadigy Kozh Woz. You're strong. No braggart can tear your arm off, or your wing. Fools and oafs. They'd make all the world into concrete and tarmac."

"West", said Link, "I'm going west."

"West, west, west" she said. "West, west, west."

Link's head appeared out of another pond – a perfect circle in a field, and a stretch of trees to the west. He sat on the edge, with a foot and a claw dangling in the water. Looking around him there was something about the lie of the land that told him he was still in knuckeridoodle land – it would have to be, because the pond was another knuckerhole. It was west of Lyminster, though, if only by a few miles. His idea of the distance between Binsted and Lyminster was fairly accurate.

Seeing light growing in the east over some woods, as sunrise began, he thought he'd temporarily resist the urge to head west and go a little way east to the woods towards Tortington.

As soon as he approached the tree line he felt the hostility. The woods were ancient – mixed woodland: oak, beech, elm, ash and yew. The trees themselves weren't necessarily ancient, though some were, they'd lived and they'd died, but this was woodland that had existed as such for a very long time.

Link felt a darkness, not dissimilar to that under Chanklebury. But he also felt the strength to resist it, and none of the claustrophobia.

Terrible things, terrible things had happened here. The civil war and bands of soldiers. People. Bloody people. The Nan Tuck's Lane stories that weren't of the otherworld, that didn't have satisfactory endings.

Link didn't feel the need to resist this hostility. He just felt an overwhelming sadness and turned back west.

That day he slept in the graveyard of Binsted Church, hidden between a tree and a wall. It felt comfortable and he felt a history around him that was more light than darkness.

Swifts darted around the church.

7: A27

The A27 is a major road in England. It runs from its junction with the A36 at Whiteparish (near Salisbury) in the county of Wiltshire. It closely parallels the south coast in Hampshire, then passes through West Sussex and terminates at Pevensey (near Eastbourne and Bexhill) in East Sussex.

A27 Road, Wikipedia

Trivia, the Roman goddess of crossroads and guardian of roads. Her name is derived from the Latin word 'Trivia' meaning 'three ways' from 'tri' meaning three and 'via' meaning way or road. In Latin, 'trivialis' appertained to the crossroads where three roads met, which came to be known, in towns, as the 'trivium', or the public place.

www.triviaholidays.eu

The goddess Arke is sometimes affiliated with the faded second rainbow sometimes seen in the shadow of the first. She is said to have iridescent wings, compared to her sister Iris's golden ones.

Arke, Wikipedia

Link looked out across knucheridoodle land that evening and flexed his claw. He felt a strain and a sharp pain in one of the devil's stitches, but the rest of his body felt washed clean, stronger. He set off across a field, always heading westwards, but, on seeing the safe darkness of woodland, he headed slightly north towards Hedger's Hill. The sound of traffic grew, until he was watching, through the trees, the vehicles hurtling along the A27. The A27 headed very clearly westwards, well, that is if it wasn't heading eastwards, and so fitted with Link's sense of direction.

So many creatures lay trails – badger paths, deer tracks, fox paths, hedgehog lines, and humans have their unconscious 'desire paths', their pedestrian shortcuts, their tracks across shrub beds or corners cut from the right angles of planned paths. But it is the deliberately planned roads of humans that seem to define their thinking; their linear narrative. Endless stretches of tarmac, on which they sit in their hurtling machines, their surroundings a blur – just background – not even a setting for the narrative, just an irrelevant fuzz glimpsed out of a window, except when a car breaks down, and the occupants find themselves placed next to some woods or a deserted industrial estate, or a bleak no-man's land on the edge of a town – suddenly centred. Suddenly somewhere. Often a nowhere-somewhere; the sort of place where Link could find refuge.

Link didn't walk, with his lopsided clip flap, on the A27 itself; he followed it from the side, so he was always in a place, centred on himself, in a somewhere alongside the road – the cars were blurs. He walked fields and plunged through hedges, or dragged himself over them. The strength he felt he had gained whilst swirling through the knuckerhole seemed to be evaporating, and his walk was getting more lopsided, the claw and the foot were too different, and he began to feel that his body was tearing up through the middle, and there was sharp pain around some of the devil's stitches. This awkward gait could help him over hedges, because he'd flop and fall and twist over them, but as he limped across fields, sometimes a feather would fall from his wing, like a quill pen being blown from a table in a scriptorium.

Near Chichester there were sports fields and fences and rough land between the A27 and the roads of housing estates, or industrial units. This rough land was full of the larva people's detritus – beer cans, sweet wrappers, wet, torn magazines, shredded tyres, used condoms, shit and tissues, polystyrene cups. These things could build a picture, a narrative; a story based on things that happen, but things that are ignored during the telling of a tale.

People's stories, thought Link, must follow a path, a road – but as it does so it gives off a cascade of stuff – a spray of detritus littering the edge of that path.

7: A27

Beyond Chichester, as Link's walk grew more lopsided, he felt his wing become almost skeletal – hollow bones aching without the protection of feathers. Each feather that fluttered away into the darkness, seemed to take a story – although Link could never quite grasp what the stories were – slippery memories, explanations. What he had tried to grasp at became ever more intangible until the only narrative he knew was the road, the endless passing of traffic, the fields and hedges and fences and ditches and lay-bys and copses and playing fields, and the debris-strewn strips and verges between housing and road.

The A27 morphed into the M27, though that meant nothing to Link. Road signs changing from green to blue, different representation on maps, different categorisations in documents – abstractions confused with actuality – as per usual. There was a line of hills again, as if the Sussex Downs were returning. Indeed it was part of the same chalk ridge, the same pile of ancient, dead, marine organisms – Portsdown Hill, overlooking Portsea Island and Portsmouth. To the left the land had dropped down to marshes, a place where Link could feel safe. His skeletal wing was hurting, he felt he needed to give up the hollow bones to the ache and the damp and let them consume it. He wanted to lie down and fragment, let the earth absorb the pieces – to become a stain on the ground like the last vestiges of a dead crow.

There was a shelter made out of concrete blocks, and in the shelter there was a man. He didn't look like one of the larva people. His beard and hair were matted and thick, his clothes filthy, and his skin the weather-beaten colour of the people at the stone, or the people of Link's fading Wealden memories. Link slumped onto the wooden bench next to the man, and the man didn't flinch. This world – the otherworld – the next – the last; the divisions started to seem more irrelevant, and, whatever world he was in, Link felt no need, and no desire, to hide himself from this fragment of humanity.

The man made a grunting sound, which sounded like "Fuck off", and Link, holding the remains of his wing with his arm, said "No".

7: A27

Both – adept at scaring people away, at filling people with disgust – accepted the other's presence and sat on the wooden bench like matching, but not identical, book ends. Link felt that he had lost the ability to walk on and just wanted to stay in a shelter between motorway and marshes. The motorway was a line clearly pointing west – but as the words slipped away from Link, he began to feel that there was no story, no reason to walk in any direction, no clippety-hoppity exhaustion, no aching at the knees; no reason to be. He would rest throughout the night, as well as the day.

The man's grunt, after an hour of dozing, could have been "What the fuck are you?" His grunting, most of which was unintelligible to any people who came across him, seemed clear enough to Link. Their conversation lasted the whole night.

They both spoke in fragments – fragments connected by a logic which flowed and merged like streams, rivers, rivulets in a catchment area – a logic only comprehensible to the two of them, but a logic that was clear if you rode upon it, if you were part of its flow.

The man seemed to make something of Link's story, even to the piecing together of parts of creatures by someone in the deep, dark, woods. He was beyond questioning and doubting, he was just hearing a story in the dark, in a shelter, in Farlington Marshes.

Nor was Link reacting against the man, he wasn't disgusted by him, as he was by the smoother larvae like people; he wasn't patronising him – he was allowing a story to flow. Link didn't have the experience of the nuances of human life to fully comprehend the man's story; but that also meant that he wouldn't recoil, wouldn't judge.

The man had joined the merchant navy when he was really no more than a boy. On his first trip, after his mother had made the big mistake of seeing him off from the quayside, he was targeted, and comprehensively sexually abused. In terms of a humane description this was an absolute catalogue of horrors; in terms of a dirty, merchant navy, poem it was a funny story told by drunk men: Harpic Shagnasty and his mates, afloat on the tossing briny.

The young man, belaboured into accepting his role on board more than just this ship, joined a 'gay scene' in Portsmouth, a scene that wasn't the slightest bit 'gay' – a violent maelstrom of pain and abuse. Of course, a variety of substances both deadened the pain, and was meant to heighten the sensations – though alcohol was the best at just dulling everything.

The man, drifting beyond his own self-disgust, floated away from any scene, gay or otherwise, like a ship with engine failure; until the only thing left was alcohol. There was just him, pissing himself out on Farlington Marshes, growing older, shambling into Pompey (Portsmouth), no longer caring whether the reaction was horror, pity or both.

His mind drifted into its own internal logic – the self-knowledge of someone who no longer gives a shit.

The morning came, and the twitchers arrived. Farlington Marshes is a great spot for bird watching, and an osprey had been spotted on the previous day, the great raptor standing by the shoreline surrounded by an avian exclusion zone, as all the other birds kept a safe distance. The osprey had flown high above clouds from North Africa, over the Mediterranean, Spain and France and the Channel and then tumbled down to spend time in the marshes by Portsmouth, taking a break, before heading for the Scottish Highlands. Feathers. When Link flapped his wing, there was never anything except feathers detaching and spiralling to the ground.

The twitchers kept a safe distance from the shelter with the wooden bench; it smelt, and they were used to the old tramp who slept there, and who was always ready to burst out into angry cursing and strings of incoherent abuse. There were some officious twitchers who complained about the way this shelter had been turned into a no-go area by a tramp, but most had the sensitivity to let it go. Anyway, there were plans afoot to demolish it, and build a visitor centre, a place to guide people around the marshes, and plan their leisure time peregrinations for them.

The man stood up and grunted and shambled towards the road into Portsmouth. There were doors he could knock on and get some food or some coins – before he returned to the same places too many times and people began to regret their kindness. He was known, the police never treated him badly; but no-one knew his story.

Link slid out of the shelter and found himself a ditch near the car park. He had learned that often the safest place to remain unseen was close to places where people gathered, before they went off to look at whatever they thought they were supposed to look at.

The man's story dug and sliced at Link's mind – it was the first time since he'd left Piltdown that a story took away his sleep in such a way; and confused the difference between the otherworld, and the world that Link had thought of as *this* world – the world by which the *other*world defined itself. Link didn't fully comprehend the nature or effects of sexual abuse, the reasons for the injuries to the man's psyche, the things that people did to each other; but he felt that there was something terrible in the human part of his construction, and within the being of that man, this terrible element of humanity had contrived to cast the man out. Strangely to Link, this made him feel less different from the people that he walked amongst, but hid from. He longed to talk to the old woman, but he felt that she was nowhere near and he felt that there was no reason he should deserve less solitude than the man.

The healing that he felt he had gained from his journey through the knuckerhole had been replaced by nothing but pain and exhaustion – but there was a whispering in his head and a surge of warmth through the hollow bones of his wing. Knucker breath. Crunch of gravel as a car pulled out of the car park.

"I'm Trivia", said the voice in his head.

"Aren't we all", grunted a sour voice that was Link's.

"Silly, silly, silly", whispered the voice. "Here there was a roadside shrine to me – Chichester to Portchester, and a road up and over the hill to the north. My crossroads. Silly creature."

"My wing is crumbling" said Link's voice in his head.

"Arke's wings were torn from her – but she grew them again. That Saxon Knucker cleaned you out – but you have to walk and you have been walking."

7: A27

There was only a pale sun in the sky, but Link felt great warmth in that wing, as he dozed on.

The sun sank into the west, and the twitchers came out to watch the hubbub of gulls, the returning Canada geese, the two barn owls, the osprey – but the osprey had flown on towards Scotland.

The man came shuffling back after the sun disappeared altogether, and the twitchers had lugged their camera equipment into their cars and driven away.

Link sat on the bench next to the man, and they both looked in surprise at Link's new iridescent feathers.

"Fuck me, an angel", said the man, "why do you only have one wing?"

Link couldn't think of an answer but spread some of the new-found warmth in his wing to the man, before setting off westwards.

8: HAGSTONE

Northam: This area includes the shores of the Northam peninsula and adjacent parts of the River Itchen. Prehistoric finds discovered in the area include a Bronze Age rapier. Roman finds have also been made. There may have been a river crossing here. The area is referred to in 842 AD as North Hamwic. The Hegestone was a medieval boundary stone. Burials were found near the stone in the 19th century. From the 17th century onwards, the waterfront was developed for shipbuilding and other industries. The River Itchen deposits preserve the remains of prehistoric landscapes and may contain the remains of maritime vessels of all periods.

Southampton City Council – Historic Environment Record Local Areas of Archaeological Potential 13/05/2010

Hagstone: a naturally perforated stone used as an amulet against witchcraft.

Merriam-Webster dictionary

The **vanishing hitchhiker** is an urban legend in which people travelling by vehicle meet with or are accompanied by a hitchhiker who subsequently vanishes without explanation, often from a moving vehicle. Vanishing hitchhikers have been reported for centuries and the story is found across the world, with many variants. The popularity and endurance of the legend has helped it spread into popular culture.

Wikipedia

Link followed the motorway

There was strange land at the edge of Portsea Island – the cut that separated Portsea Island, a slab of land stuffed full of Portsmouth, from the housing spreading up to the base of Portsdown Hill. There was scrubland and muddy creek, and a larger version of the human throw-away/cast off/detritus strip that always seemed to lie beside the more substantial roads. Then Portsmouth was gone, the road rose to meet Portsdown Hill, as the hill faded away to meet the road.

Link was back in the familiar territory of field and woodland, small housing estates and industrial units. He passed tunnels under the motorway, tunnels for roads and tunnels for pedestrian paths, tunnels for drainage, tunnels for murky, bubbling water, for places and spaces, occasional people and faces… and Link sometimes watched his feathers glow – having absorbed sunlight in the places he hid during the day, at night they fed warmth into his blood – and shone each time he felt a fresh surge of encouragement.

Always there was the roar of traffic from the M27.

The motorway bridged a river and Link sat by the side of the river, watching a rippled reflection of the moon and feeling the coldness of the water between his toes and through his foot, whilst feeling an uncomfortable nothing through his claw.

Some of his feathers picked up the moonlight and glowed a soft blue. Link looked up at the concrete bridge arching over the river and felt a reluctance to climb onto it and walk the hard shoulder. Possibly people would see him, people already had, though they had just glimpsed something dark, out of the corner of the eye, as the car sped past. Maybe a soft moon-glow from his feathers would draw attention to that briefly noticed silhouette, but it was an uncomfortable place to walk anyway; noisy, dangerous, exhausting – and the feeling of being contemptuously dismissed by the larva people was greater than usual; the exclusion as they flashed by in their cars.

The motorway was still heading west, but also curving northwards, in order to avoid the city that lay ahead. Link turned away from the bridge and the road and started southwards along the edge of the estuarine river – shingle, washed-up plastic, driftwood – then he came to the chain link fence of the Air Traffic Control Centre. He solemnly examined the face of a CCTV camera that stared rudely back at him, recording, somewhere, an image of feathers and stitched skin and questing eyes.

Link reached a Victorian bridge over a railway cutting. Somewhere in Link's head the devil rhapsodised about railway timetables and lists of railway station names. An old woman stood on the bridge, in a cloud of smoke as a steam train chugged beneath. She was lighting a clay pipe and, as she did so, she was transformed into a pillar of flame. "Spontaneous combustion", said the voice in Link's head – maybe the voice was Lord Moon's, percolating through Link's body from moonlit feathers, through the hollow bones of the wing, and up to his head. "The old woman, old Polly, was so soaked in alcohol, that when she lit her pipe, she combusted. It was a well-known story."

"Bloody stories", thought Link, as the vision faded and a late-night diesel commuter train, too late for commuters, clattered beneath the bridge. Link followed the cutting until the railway rose to the surface and crossed the river on a metal bridge, parallel to the motorway.

As the motorway arched away north-westwards, Link followed the railway into Southampton. It was an erratic route, twisting and turning through the city, and Link was tempted to leave the railway and head directly west – but there were no ways, no paths or tracks that did that, and the land around the railway felt safe and secure. Foxes and badgers used it, it was an unbroken corridor into the city; saplings seeded and grew, trees created tangles of roots and stems and suckers. The railway corridor was an artefact, planned and created by people, but it allowed in the unplanned; the random.

Link could see, from the railway, as it twisted into Southampton, another river, wide and meandering – he could see it by the lights of the city centre on the far bank, by the blue lights of a long, arching road bridge, and strands of lights from flats, streets and houses, on both sides. He followed the railway along the eastern side of the river, crossed another bridge, came to a railway junction, after which he found himself heading back down the river on the western side. Now he had to keep clear of the track;

long, heavy goods trains roared and rattled past; the locomotive a flash of light, and then a long line of trucks: dark, devoid of life.

As the railway diverged from the river, he left it at a level crossing, and followed the water, on a track next to an industrial estate. A large Polish articulated lorry sat behind a chain link fence, with a picture of a figure on the side of the cargo trailer; a figure composed of sausages, vegetables, haunches of meat and pickled gherkins. Link gazed at it; he'd seen many of the weird symbols of the larva people and just accepted their presence rather than wondering or questioning, but this one caused him to pause.

Then he was under a concrete bridge that carried a road over the river – there was graffiti, the drip drop of condensation, the sound of the occasional car above him, the cry of an oystercatcher flying up the river from Southampton Water, the distant sound of a police siren.

Link's feathers glowed – he felt the presence of a host of figures drifting down the river.

"They were all here, drifting down, and rowing up the river", said the old woman.

Link turned in astonishment, as the bridge faded away, and he saw mud flats bordering a lazy, meandering estuary. The old woman walked down the side of the river and Link trailed behind her, till they came to a rickety-rackety wooden shack, next to a small standing stone with a hole in it.

"Well, monster", she said, "your feathers glow. You've found something."

"Do you walk ahead of me? Did you overtake me?" asked Link, knowing that the question was unanswerable.

"Don't be silly", she said, "Look, this is the hegestone." She gestured towards the holed stone. "Look through the hole."

Link did: he saw a hill with a tower on the top. He looked up and saw the first light of morning in the east, the eastern side of the river was hillside covered in forest; the city had disappeared. He followed the old woman into the familiar hut – and sat down. As hoped for, she started to ladle out some Jerusalem artichoke soup.

"What did you see through the hole?"

"A hill with a tower. Is that Glastonbury?"

"It could well be – but you're not there yet."

"I feel stronger than I have done", said Link, "but it all seems such a long way."

"Well, you're not so very far from Hag Hill now; you can get your directions there."

"Hag Hill", said Link, "Is that your hill, you bloody old hag?"

"You monster" she spat back, "You're all bits and pieces of bloody old rubbish", but she was amused.

"How do I find Hag Hill?"

"Oh, head west, follow the railway and the not railway."

"The not railway?"

"You'll see."

"Where are we now?"

"Ah – The Millstone Marshes. I stay here in a whole shifting tide of stories. Those Jutes paddling their boats up the lazy river, watching the woods like hawks – wondering who might be lurking there. The girl climbing into the bows of the ferry, whilst the ferryman rows across the river with his back to her, so that when the boat reaches the other side, he turns round and she's vanished. Then, hundreds of years later, when there's a bridge, she hitches a lift from a couple, who, worried about a young girl hitch-hiking on a dark and rainy night, give her a lift home – only to find that she's vanished from the back seat of the car. Same girl, same river.

And all of those people, those ghosts, winners and losers, soldiers going to Agincourt, sailors carrying the bubonic plague from Marseilles, Castillian raiders including that old bastard, Grimaldi, the people sucked in by the cities growing industry, the shipyard workers, the soap factory workers, all those folk who sank with the Titanic, the folk who died under German bombs, a great multitude of them, all led by young Richard Parker of Itchen Ferry village."

"Who's he?"

"Oh, he got eaten by his shipmates. They were hungry. Adrift in an open boat."

"Out there – on the river?"

"No, you silly monster, in the South Atlantic."

The South Atlantic sounded like it was a very long way away – further than Piltdown.

Link stayed a few days with the old woman in the Millstone Marshes – she still had the jackdaw with her, but thankfully no Lord Moon. He looked through the eye of the Hegestone every so often, though in his head it was always the Hagstone, and usually saw a hill with a tower, though sometimes it was more like a low, stone building than a tower. Occasionally he saw the sea, waves and foam and bottle-green depths, and once he saw a creature that seemed to be a composite of parts from different creatures – as he was – but this had a woman's torso, a fish's tail, and a strange flat face with a mouth like a slit, out of which came a flickering snake's tongue. Link didn't think deeply about these things, he wasn't analytical, he let them roll around in his mind like the rest of the phenomena that came his way; the devil on an iron throne, hills that swallowed you whole, cars flashing past, cars hitting roundabouts and turning upside down, wide valleys, knuckerholes, railway trains, waste food behind supermarkets, Lord Moon, pink trainers, a man alone – separated from the rest of humanity, lorries with pictures of creatures made out of food, ghosts on a river.

The evening when Link set off again lacked the sadness of the time he left Amberley Wild Brooks; everything seemed perfectly natural. He assumed he would be seeing the old woman again at Hag Hill, and a Southampton "see y'later" would have been the most appropriate goodbye to say, had he known it. As he headed northwards up the river again, the Millstone Marshes faded into a small yacht marina, there were buildings and a scrap yard along the riverside, and once again Link was under the road bridge; Northam Bridge. He walked – his strange lurching, rolling walk – into a road with terraced houses along one side, and, on the other side, between the railway and the road, a Hindu Temple – Link didn't particularly differentiate it from other buildings, though an elephant-faced God in a window could have made it seem different – and then a patch of allotments.

Most of the front windows of the houses, looking directly out onto the road, had drawn curtains, but from one there was a flood of light, and a man, sitting at a desk, writing. Link felt himself ceasing to exist.

"I'm nothing. This is someone else's story. There is no me – no old woman – no Tadig Kozh; the man who was supposed to have created me. Just some bloody bloke at a desk in Northam."

"Stop it", I wrote; I'm looking out of the window and I can't see you. I can see a drunk man lurching along in the other direction. I don't want to be in the story. I can see the illuminated sign on the Siemens train care facility, a sign constantly reminding me of that company's inglorious history, and I can imagine a dark figure, a shape, a presence, clambering over the fence between the allotments and the railway yard. I can imagine Old Vic puzzling over the strange foot and claw prints crossing his allotment. He'll tell me about them. This isn't supposed to happen. Go away.

Link resumed his existence as he moved further from the malign influence of the man in the window. His feathers picked up a blue glow from the illuminated sign – and he was heading westwards by the side of the railway line, through a cutting, through a tunnel, through a station – and into the corridor of tangled trees and undergrowth that led out of the city, past docks and marshes, and into the inappropriately named New Forest; a forest very much more ancient than most.

Hag Hill. He had to go there.

9: HAG HILL AND BURLEY BEACON

Hag Hill from the path along the disused railway line. There is a car park over the brow of the hill, at intervals dog-walkers emerge onto the heathland. There are proposals to put the electricity power lines underground.

http://bit.ly/pilgrim01

The grandest concentration of Neolithic passage tombs in Ireland can be found at Loughcrew. Local folklore maintains that the site is the work of the 'monster woman' who once ruled the area. Its name in Irish is Sliabh na Callaí meaning 'Hill of the Witch' or 'Hag's Hill'. The name of the ancient hag was Garavogue, known locally as An Cailleach Bhéara. This witch or hag may have had her origins in the Celtic goddess Buí, whom we encounter at Knowth in Brú na Bóinne. She was a Moon Goddess or Earth Mother. She was a supernatural figure responsible for the landscape; placing large boulders in rivers and creating rock formations on hillsides.

http://bit.ly/pilgrim11

The **Amesbury Archer** is an early Bronze Age man whose grave was discovered during excavations at the site of a new housing development (grid reference SU16324043) in Amesbury near Stonehenge. The grave was uncovered in May 2002, and the man is believed to date from about 2,300 BC. He is nicknamed 'the Archer' because of the many arrowheads that were among the artefacts buried with him.

https://en.wikipedia.org/wiki/Amesbury_Archer

Just past Ashurst, the railway turned sharply south, and Link wondered whether he should leave it. Unlike his experience in Southampton, there would be no problem walking directly westwards – there were roads and tracks, and the New Forest itself was composed, not just of trees, but of moorland, and heath, and blanket bog – all open – a comfortable place for Link. He wondered if leaving it would mean following the 'not railway', but if everything that wasn't railway was 'not railway', it would seem to be a bit of a pointless phrase, and not a turn of speech that someone as direct as the old woman would use. So Link continued to follow the railway line, and felt better when it turned sharply westwards again, entering woodland between Woodfidley and Moon Hill. As the railway skirted the edge of Brockenhurst however, it once again turned southwards, and Link's feathers started to glow an urgent red, and that pull to the west became stronger. Then there was a bridge, taking a road over the railway, after which the railway forked off in two directions, one south-easterly and one south-westerly. Link followed the south-westerly one, but then felt something else, a sharp twinge – a pull directly to the west. He saw two fences converge, creating a point, a seemingly pointless point, and another embankment, covered in birch and alder trees. There had been a third railway line and suddenly it was clear what the old woman had meant. That railway was now gone. It had forked west and it was now possible to follow the course of the old railway line – the not railway – firstly through a tangle of trees, but then it opened out, marching over Blackhamsley Hill and Hinchelsea Bog, crossing the long, shallow, descending valley of Long Slade Bottom until Link knew that Hag Hill was on his right.

It wasn't a dramatic hill – more of a slope – nothing with a defined summit. There was a gorse bush waving at him, picked out by a strange, vagrant wind; eddying around the hill, it gestured him up the slope. Link's feathers tingled and glowed and for the first time he had feeling in the claw – a sort of sharp, sudden, twitching, as if the claw was beating time to music. As Link turned up the hill, it was the claw that was dragging the foot.

He felt he was on the top, zig-zagging amongst gorse bushes, treading a pattern within a circle, lurching from claw to foot, dancing. Down he spiralled – into the hill – spiralling widdershins. He looked for the old woman – there she was – hopping, jumping, performing a dance that was as awkward and lurching as his. He tried to greet her, but it wasn't her; the woman's face was expressionless, the eyes blank. She danced on. In the centre of the hill was the devil, sitting on an iron throne. Cloven hooves, goat's horns, goat's legs, goat's twizzle. It wasn't the devil of Tunbridge Wells, the devil of the Devil's Dyke, the devil being dragged under Chanklebury, the devil in knuckeridoodle land. It was a blank-faced devil, expressionless, breathing fire from his nostrils like a blow torch. The music was louder: it was fiddles and flutes and harps and accordions and trumpets and trombones and water swirling into guttering stand-pipes and fast running streams and rocks bouncing down steep slopes and waves crashing on the shore and sucking back the pebbles and the boom of the sea in a cave and the spray of water up a blow hole.

Then there was a circle of copper-faced people, holding hands, dancing around the inside of the hill, dancing knock-kneed and bow-legged. Charcoal burners, snake catchers, forest farmers and squatters and commoners, railway building navvies, turf-cutting women.

Behind them, another circle, whirling in the opposite direction, also holding hands, men wearing hi-viz jackets, with traffic cones on their heads. One of them burst through the whirling circles, and jumping onto a plinth next to the devil's throne, started to sing:

Heads, shoulders, knees and toes.
Knees and toes,
Aggregates and Binders,
Aggregates and Binders,
Heads, shoulders, knees and toes,
Knees and Toes
Skid resistance,
Multiple hazard,
Skid resistance,
Multiple hazard.
Arms and legs and mouth and nose,
Wing, feather and claw,
Wing and claw.

And then, dancing with Link, there was a dragon – in some ways like the Lyminster Knucker, but with fire rather than water. As it swirled and whirled, in circles and plumes of flame, it shouted, over the din, "You were expected – where are you going?"

"Glastonbury", shouted Link, "Can you show me the way?"

"Hang on", bellowed the dragon, "Hang on to my back."

The dragon spiralled up, out of the dancing circles, out of the hill – up into the sky, trailing sparks and flames – then it swooped down onto the 'not railway', the old track, and it was a steam train, hissing steam and sparks, enveloped in smoke; and Link had two arms and a shovel and was pitching coal into the firebox, and there were memories of Wealden blast furnaces, and the dragon engine whistled and puffed and shrieked full tilt across Holmsley Bog, and shouted "The next not station is Burley, Burley not station, Burley not station. Prepare to alight."

Link, alighting from the engine amidst a cloud of steam, found himself once again with an arm and a wing, as the steam engine became a dragon again, albeit a rather neat spaniel-sized dragon, and the two of them skirted the woods and the gardens around the edge of Burley, and climbed a hill, threading through oak and beech trees. They passed a large, white, house under construction, and the dragon stopped and glared.

"Monstrosity", it muttered, "money can get you round planning permission anywhere; even here."

Of course Link didn't know what the dragon was talking about, but he'd seen enough that night not to go asking questions.

"This is Burley Beacon", said the dragon, "I'm not going to be able to go any further."

Link felt a surge of disappointment; he'd hoped that the dragon, whether or not as a steam engine, would take him to Glastonbury.

Sensing his thought, the dragon said, "I'm sorry, but I can't cross the perambulation, I can't leave the forest".

They settled down amongst the trees, looking westwards over bog land, as the sun rose behind them; and the view to the west, slowly, hazily, became visible.

"The perambulation?" asked Link.

"It's the imaginary line around the New Forest, it marks the area, and I can't cross it."

"But, if it's imaginary, why can't you cross it?"

"Because it's a story – what am I? If that's the story – that's the story. Of course, in *the* story, I did cross it."

Link sensed a "Once upon a time".

"You dance under Hag Hill, you fly into the sky, you turn into a steam engine, but you can't cross an imaginary line. There must be a 'Once upon a time'."

"A bit ordinary, really", said the dragon, who was slowly inflating to a more dragon-like size, "The usual dragon story; nothing as wonderful as steaming up the Burley line, whistle tooting, wheels clattering. Once upon a time I was a dragon – up here, on the Beacon. I was fed up with eating hedgehogs and badgers – though venison was always good, as was wild boar – though the wild boar used to fight back. Down in the valley, though, down there..."

Link looked down, past the bog land, and into the greenness of the Hampshire Avon Valley. The rising sun was evaporating the night dew, and swirls of mist were rising from the water meadows.

"... Down there, I could see cattle and sheep and goats and pigs – but it was the wrong side of the perambulation. I couldn't cross it. At least I thought I couldn't. But after a particularly nasty wild boar had charged me from behind and punctured more than my pride, I'd just had enough. I soared up into the air, crossed the perambulation – and nothing happened. So I raided Lower Bisterne Farm, and discovered that all those animals, the livestock, were just unbelievably delicious. I took to raiding all the farms between Blissford and Winkton until the whole place was in uproar. Well, it's the usual story: they called a knight, Sir Maurice de Berkeley, a loud-mouthed dragon slayer, to come and do battle. He plastered his armour with bird lime and covered the bird lime with broken glass. Vicious. I squeezed him, the glass cut into me; three days, three nights, we fought, and then he cut off my head. He died shortly afterwards – that's the usual story too. But where my blood flowed there's a circular patch on the ground where nothing will ever grow."

Link started.

"Is it the same circle on the ground – is it the one there always is?"

The dragon looked surprised.

"You mean when they kill a dragon?"

"No – any story. Where the people killed the girl. Where the old woman had a rickety-rackety wooden shack."

"I wouldn't know, but there's always one where a knight kills a dragon. Saint bloody George of course, St Efflam, the Blessed bloody Ammon, John frigging Lambton, St. Murrough O'Heany (he used cheap tricks), St Michael – he always killed them on hills, after which they'd build churches."

A picture of a church on a hill flashed across Link's mind.

"Dragon slayers – they can't cope with the old stories, so they kill them and make up new ones."

"I think whoever made me is on a hill" said Link, "It might be Glastonbury."

"Ah yes, of course", said the dragon, "if I were you I'd follow Guinevere's funeral cortege, that'll get you to Glastonbury."

"Guinevere?"

"The old queen of England, or Wessex, or Britain, or storyland – or some such. She died in Amesbury Abbey but she had to be buried with her husband, Arthur, in Glastonbury. The funeral cortege is always travelling from Amesbury to Glastonbury, along old Woden's Dyke."

Link wasn't following all of this, but he seized upon the prospect of a whole company guiding him to Glastonbury.

You'll have to get to Amesbury first, said the dragon.

"Could you please…?"

"You know I can't cross the perambulation… yes, I know I did before, and look what happened. I'm not repeating that story again."

The dragon pointed his tail in a northerly direction.

"That way. Down to the Avon Valley – down to Lower Bisterne Farm and Crow; watch out for knights in armour and follow the A338."

Link looked with dismay across the Avon valley, and into a blue distance. What was the chance of happening directly onto Amesbury?

"Stonehenge" said the dragon, "all of us dragons know about that. Mystical, schmystical, twistical – worse than your bloody Glastonbury. I can stamp the perfect dragon-tracking system on that for you; any piece of myth or legend can find that place, even poor fictitious Tess Durbeyfield."

The dragon poked Link with his tail.

"Ouch", said Link and felt a queasy feeling as his sense of direction adjusted itself and narrowed down to something more specifically focused.

There were plenty of others who had headed in this direction, Link felt a throng behind him, ready to push him on – and many of them had walked a good deal further than he had.

"The Amesbury Archer", said the dragon, "he walked from Switzerland."

"Good for him", thought Link, feeling a surge of self-pity, "if he was an archer, he knew he was an archer, I don't know what I am."

"Good luck", called the dragon, as Link set off down the hill.

Link felt that his life was entirely comprised of leaving – goodbye, goodbye, goodbye. Just start to feel comfortable; then off you go. He thought of the man in the shelter on Farlington Marshes and wondered again.

With the weight of an invisible throng of pilgrims behind him, he headed off down the slope. Crossing Cranes Moor, he looked round, and back up to Burley Beacon. There were flames – they were coming from the new white house – the form of a dragon flapped around the hill and disappeared into the woodland.

As Link reached the perambulation of the New Forest, he heard the siren of the fire engine rushing in from Ringwood.

10: GUINEVERE'S FUNERAL CORTEGE

And there was ordained an horse bier; and so with an hundred torches ever burning around the corpse of the queen, and ever Sir Lancelot with his seven fellows went about the horse bier, singing and reading many an holy orison, and frankincense upon the corpse incensed. Thus Sir Lancelot and his seven fellows went on foot from Almesbury unto Glastonbury.

Sir Thomas Malory, *Le Morte D'Arthur*

And there have been various sightings of a spectral funeral cortege processing along the Wansdyke at night, a golden crown placed upon the coffin; this has been linked with the body of Guinevere being taken from Amesbury (by a somewhat roundabout route, it must be confessed) to Glastonbury.

John Chandler, *The Vale of Pewsey*

"You can see it on the skyline from the garden of the Barge Inn."

Teaching Assistant in local school

"Many years passed, and I went back again
Among those villages, and looked for men
Who might have known my ancient. He himself
Had long been dead or laid upon the shelf,
I thought. One man I asked about him roared
At my description: 'Tis old Bottlesford
He means, Bill.' But another said: 'Of course,
It was Jack Button up at the White Horse.
He's dead, sir, these three years.' This lasted till
A girl proposed Walker of Walker's Hill,
'Old Adam Walker. Adam's Point you'll see
Marked on the maps.'

Edward Thomas, 'Lob'

Link plodded north-west, and then north, walking parallel to a road as so often before. He felt that his sense of direction, like the pointer in a liquid-based compass, kept drifting back to its former alignment, but then shifted to the Stonehenge route under the influence of a shadowy cloud of dead pilgrims. It felt at times as if there was a mist enveloping him, and the pilgrimage felt as nebulous as the mist; he felt that his church on a hill destination was being lost.

He left the vicinity of the road and climbed hills to the west of Salisbury. Dozing in a thicket during the day time, he gazed out in wonder at the cathedral spire in the distance. He thought of towers and rockets and arrows, and, looking at what seemed to be such a big sky behind it, flapped his one wing, and wished that he had two, and could fly up to the great cumulus clouds.

A little further north he came to the River Bourne and followed it, but the pilgrim cloud started to agitate, it seemed now to be comprised of oscillating particles – all wanting to pull him back to the northward route that the river, flowing westwards, was taking him away from. As Link approached the stark security fence and buildings of the Porton Down Research Facility, he heard tiny voices from the cloud, and he felt their fear. If people caught a glimpse of Link it was them who would usually react with fear, though Link trudged through their landscape, avoiding their lethal vehicles, passing their buildings, surmounting their obstacles. Now he felt a great fear of people, of what they did and could do, of the darkness of their minds lurking and skulking in these desolate buildings.

He followed the agitating pilgrim cloud across fields, and as they calmed down, he found himself in Amesbury. The cloud whiffled off westwards to Stonehenge and Link was left sitting behind the giant wheelie bins in a car park.

He spent the day there – and in the evening there was a clatter of skate boards and a hubbub of voices. After a while it calmed down, and then, near the bins, there were the voices of older youths.

"I'll get a fucking squaddie and slam his head on the ground. Fucking mash him." There was laughter.

"Fucking kick the shit out of him – slam his head on the ground again."

The voice appeared to be winding itself up into a frenzy. The others were laughing and spitting aggression at the same time. Link didn't know who it was directed against, or how people could, at the same time, combine rage with laughter. He felt that those elements were within himself and he didn't know what to do with them. He got up, crashed out into the car park from between the bins, raised his wing, and squealed like a wild boar. The young men, and one young woman, stared at him open mouthed, as Link shook himself like a wet dog, or a bird that had just taken a bath in a puddle, and, as he squealed again, they turned and ran.

He wandered darkening Amesbury, not knowing what was an abbey and what was a supermarket. Then, faintly at first, but getting louder and louder, he heard the sound of trumpets, the beating of drums, the screeching of clarinets, the oompah of trombones, and round the corner came the band. The men dressed in blazers, ties, and striped trousers, and a huge woman all wrapped around with a tuba. There were four men, all wearing dark glasses, even though it was dark anyway, and they had dancing footsteps, and they were carrying a coffin with a golden crown set on top of it.

"The otherworld" thought Link, "the other than the otherworld – all mixed up now – though not always seeing each other. The story of the story – surely what is 'real' has no story; it's just there. The warmth of the sun, the stink of the bins."

The large woman, who was wearing a tight dress, and who danced with lurching, funereal footsteps, gestured, with a tilt of her head, for Link to join them. The beat of the big, bass drum, the rattle of the snare drums, the oompah of the big trombone, the rhythm of the marching, dancing feet – all lifted Link's spirits, and he marched, in his twisting way, out of Amesbury. Northwards out of town they marched:

10: GUINEVERE'S FUNERAL CORTEGE

Milston, Ablington, Fittleton, Coombe
Milston, Ablington, Fittleton, Coombe
Pomp pom pom went the big bass drum.

Just shadows to any cars that drove along the minor roads, as the cars were shadows to them; just shadows to anyone looking out of their night-time windows; the procession, danced and marched towards the Vale of Pewsey and the dark ridge of the Pewsey Hills: the Marlborough Downs.

After crossing the Kennet and Avon canal at Honeystreet, the funeral cortege started to ascend the slope of Golden Ball Hill. As they did so, there was a bang, and the coffin lid burst open, sending the crown spinning. A dancing mourner caught the crown and started to play it like a tambourine.

Guinevere sat up, lifted her arms; there was the whoop of a siren whistle and Guinevere's head moved rapidly and mechanically from side to side.

"Arthur, my Arthur", she screamed, "I'm coming to you."

"Arthur, Arthur, we're coming to you" shouted the trombone player.

"Arthur, Arthur, we're coming to you" howled the trumpet player.

"Arthur, Arthur, we're coming to you" bellowed the man with the big, bass drum.

The juggler and the clown screamed "Arthur, Arthur, we're coming to you."

The fire eater blew out a ball of flame, "Arthur, Arthur, we're coming to you."

Guinevere looked at Link, with a face as blank as that of the devil or the old woman under Hag Hill.

"Lancelot, Lancelot, kiss me no more", she screeched, then lay back with a sudden jerk, as the coffin lid banged shut and a siren whistle wailed.

Link wondered whether he was called Lancelot, but didn't like the name very much.

Up to the ridge they marched, and then danced along the skyline, over Knap Hill and Walker's Hill, after which they sank down into Adam's Grave long barrow. Inside the hill there lay a sleeping giant made of mud. It seemed to contain some form of life; there was a gentle snoring coming from its mud-bubbling mouth. Link thought of his own consciousness seeping into him, as he lay on a woodland floor at Piltdown, and looking around at the other members of the funeral cortege for some sort of explanation or story, he saw that they were all mud – chalky mud – bubbling mouths, flints and shepherd's crowns, fossil echinoids for eyes.

The next evening they were out of the hill, and off again, as the mud giant slumbered on. Along the ridge of Milk Hill they danced, visible from the vale below to those who see such things; from Honeystreet and Alton Barnes, from Stanton St. Bernard and All Cannings; visible as silhouettes against a darkening, northerly sky; enlarged to the size of evening shadows, like a row of dancing shadow puppets.

Onto Woden's Dyke, the Wansdyke, they danced; over Tan Hill and Roughbridge Hill – over ups and downs – over All Cannings Down and Allington Down and Easton Down and Horton Down, with their long barrows and sleeping giants; over Bishops Cannings Down and uppity-down, and up – up past the enigmatic radio masts of Morgan's Hill, and down into the flat land beyond Stockley.

At this point they began to follow a Roman road that no longer existed – the road to the lead mines of Charterhouse-on-Mendip – a road to a terrible place of smoke and flame and slavery – a place harder even than the iron works of the Weald that held such a prominent place in Link's fractured memory. When they marched, marched and danced, they were just a vapour, swiffling through villages and farms, through walls and buildings, walking on levels above the ground, or wading chest-deep through ground, walking a 1st-century geography, through a 21st-century landscape. Marching through fields, chest-deep across roads, marching through the middle of the Odd Down Sainsburys, through the aisles of wine and beer, through the staff room, across the car park, all during the night. Invisible, yet sometimes giving a security guard or a late-night reveller staggering home, a 'someone's walked across my grave' feeling, a twinge of goose pimples.

In the day time Link slept back in the 21st-century landscape, hidden in ditches, or copses, or garden sheds, or behind bins, or in those fragments of land in urban places, hollows enclosed by rusty fences, hollows full of sycamore and silver birch and polluted streams and accumulated litter. Whilst he dozed, the funeral cortege swirled around him like cigarette smoke.

Then there was the massif of the Mendip hills and Link felt the exhilaration of climbing up to heights again. All this time, his legs, his foot, his claw never ached, his stitches were fading, the feathers on his wing were glossy, his eyes shone.

East of Charterhouse the party abruptly abandoned the Roman road, and the 1st-century geography of that road, and turned south to Priddy, gleefully circling, seven times, the pile of hurdles that sit permanently on the triangular green. Then, just south of Priddy, Link, looking out from the high Mendips, across the low-lying flat land of the Somerset Levels, caught his first glimpse of Glastonbury Tor. His heart – his charcoal burner's heart, his corvid bird heart, his badger heart, his wild boar heart – leapt. That pinnacle, standing alone in the amphitheatre between the Mendips, the Quantocks, and the Bristol Channel, the tower on the top – St. Michael's Tower, St. Michael the dragon slayer, mist swirling around the base of the tor, this must be it, the place. Tadig Kozh, his creator, would be there. The whole point of his story would be there. Surely.

The cortege clambered down the cool, mossy, crevice of Ebbor Gorge and slept that day in Wookey Hole, whilst visitors from Bristol and Birmingham passed them and stared at the stone witch, and the stalagmites and stalactites, never noticing a funeral cortege eddying around the rocks like vapour, or Link sleeping unseen in the shadows.

11: GLASTONBURY AND THE LEVELS

"Glastonbury Abbey was renowned in the middle ages as the reputed burial place of the legendary King Arthur and the site of the earliest church in Britain, thought to have been founded by Joseph of Arimathea. ...The monks needed to raise money by increasing the numbers of visiting pilgrims – and that meant keeping the myths and legends alive."

Prof Roberta Gilchrist, Glastonbury Abbey Archaeological Archive Project, 2016

"The cakes neglected by King Alfred, supposedly because he was immersed in thought about how to rescue Britain from the Vikings, were stolen from a Norse saga in which they were used to extol Ragnar Hairybreeks, a notorious harrier of the Anglo-Saxons. ... The blatant stealing of the story to serve Alfred's reputation came more than 100 years later in a monkish chronicle that turned the loaves into cakes and Ragnar's bride into a swineherd's wife who berates the king with democratic gusto", said Professor Rory McTurk.

The Guardian: http://bit.ly/pilgrim21

Through Wells, and into Glastonbury, Link felt his heart rising. He knew his feathers were shining – he felt that he was approaching the climax of a story. As they approached a medieval ruin, cut grass and information boards, the coffin lid burst open again, and Guinevere shot upright like a jack in a box.

"Arthur, I come to you", she screeched. The band blew a fanfare, the fire-eater blew out a ball of fire and, as if they'd come to the end of a huge elastic band after stretching it as far as possible, they all shot back eastwards, leaving Link standing, solitary, baffled, bereft. He stumbled a few steps back, but he felt no sense of their presence, and he imagined the cortege way back in Amesbury, starting out all over again. His feeling of making progress, of purposeful travel, evaporated. He climbed into the grounds of Glastonbury Abbey and wandered aimlessly.

"Arthur, I come to you", he tried to say, hoping that, as an incantation, it would cause something to happen – but all that came out was a squeal. Remembering what Guinevere had called him, he tried to say, "It is I, Lancelot", but there was just another squeal, and he felt the words were foolish anyway. He clambered out into Chilkwell Street and, feeling the presence of the tor ahead of him in the darkness, he lurched towards it. Something had gone from him with the sudden disappearance of Guinevere's funeral cortege, but he gathered hope up inside himself, as he saw the darkness of the hill rising ahead. "Tadig Kozh, be there. Please be there", he thought, and then felt that his thought sounded as pathetic as a marionette queen screaming, "Arthur, I come to you."

Turning past Chalice Well he started up the hill, lying down flat in the grass when a man in robes passed, circling the hill and chanting softly. On reaching the hollow Saint Michael's Tower at the top of the tor, Link felt a surge of hope. Moving from one entrance of the tower to the other he looked out at the lights of Glastonbury in one direction, and, from the other side, lights from the scattered villages of the Somerset Levels. He spread-eagled himself face down on the ground within the tower, waiting to sink into the otherworld, the underworld, the world under the hill.

He didn't.

He wondered if the flagstones were preventing him from sinking downwards, so he stumbled outside, and lay on the grass. He tried to wish himself into the hill – he was himself at Piltdown again, mouth full of soil and stone. He didn't even feel that there was anything beneath him. A blankness. Limestone, mudstone, sandstone. The crushed solid forms of ancient life. He almost wished for the dismal, depressive claustrophobia of Chanklebury – there wasn't even that – this nothingness felt worse. Lonely. No meaning.

The chanting man reached the top of the hill and Link sat up with a sudden surge of annoyance. The man's mouth dropped open, he stopped chanting, and slowly retreated backwards.

"Are you...? Are you...?" stammered the man. Link squealed and the man turned and descended the tor in a straight line – circumambulations abruptly abandoned.

Link miserably left the tor before sunrise. A straggle of people ascended the hill from Chalice Well but Link, heading at first for neighbouring Wearyall Hill, sought sanctuary in a retail park next to a roundabout. He climbed a chain link fence and hid himself amongst wooden pallets in the service area of B&Q.

Each night he returned to the tor, and people began to catch glimpses of him. Usually these were just fleeting impressions of something strange and dark, accompanied by an animal smell – but a woman who was rather fond of hallucinogenic mushrooms, and who slept in a tent that she moved around the base of the tor, stood directly in front of him and tried to engage him in conversation. She backed away, more because of his smell than the sight of him, though she was hardly fragrant herself. Link, frustrated by his inability to communicate in this mundane world, wondered how he had communicated with the man in Farlington Marshes – he had to achieve a pattern, a mode of speech that involved following a flow, like water in a stream. He couldn't create that deliberately, it just had to happen. The woman and Link backed away from each other and both fled.

In the day he mostly hid in the retail park, in the service areas of B&Q and Tesco; one time, as Link lay behind the bins, the bin lorry arrived, and the bin men saw something dark haul itself around a corner. Sometimes he hid in sheds in the gardens of houses around the base of Wearyall Hill or in cluttered yards at the backs of the esoteric, new-age knick-knack shops of Glastonbury, or in builders' yards at the beginning of the Meare Road that led out to the Levels. One day he slept behind trees at the edge of the playing fields of exclusive Millfield School and listened to a little boy crying with loneliness and muttering in

Russian. Link felt an echo of that desolation, a desolation made greater by his helplessness, as he remained hidden.

On the march to Glastonbury he had felt that the stitches put in by the devil had dissolved away as the wounds had healed, but now he felt them again, and he felt threads straining and snapping as wounds reopened. His feathers lost their gloss and started to spiral away, and his one arm ached from the extra strain put on it by the lack of another arm to balance and equalise its burden.

Link was losing stories. The feathers took memories, bits and pieces of Once upon a time, tales and histories; there was just him and this dismal town. The hiding and scavenging brought back one memory, that of being in the same position in Steyning and always looking up at a dominating hill; and the horror of Chanklebury seemed to be surpassed by the empty oblivion of Glastonbury Tor.

One night, as Link lay at the top of the tor, a policeman and woman ascended the hill. Link could hear, on the still night air, the voices of people talking, arguing – haranguing the two police.

"It's up there", said one.

"Let it be, blessed be", said the voice of the woman with the tent.

"There is something", said another, "it is scary – I don't mind stuff round here; but can't have someone frightening the shit out of everyone."

The woman said something else; "You're all right, love", said a male voice in a patronising manner, "but we don't know who this is."

The two police had already abandoned the vocal throng and were further up the tor. Link had had enough. He finally abandoned the tor, and descending the other side, crossed a field and clambered over a hedge into Basketfield Lane. Circling the tor at a distance, he headed back through Glastonbury, and out to the Meare Road, the road to the flat land he'd seen from both the tor and the Mendips; the Levels. It felt like a reminder of Amberley Wild Brooks – a place of refuge – maybe even a hope of finding the old woman.

11: GLASTONBURY AND THE LEVELS

There was some stuff bubbling around on social media now; though nothing to be taken too seriously, given it's fusing with all the usual Glastonbury 'spiritual' stuff. The policeman and woman engaged in a certain amount of good-natured workplace banter with their colleagues, though they both felt that something had been up there – someone who needed a good bath anyway; but then, that wasn't unusual. In Worthing, though, on the Sussex coast, an obsessed young man, with several computers, started drawing lines between sightings, on a map. It was a long, straight, line that leads from Amesbury to Glastonbury – and it touched neither the Vale of Pewsey nor the Mendips.

The Somerset Levels were a comfortable place for Link, a place where he no longer felt himself to be falling apart, but neither was he healing – his feathers didn't glow with optimism – he was at a sort of stasis, a wounded creature of the Levels; in his isolation, almost a king.

Summer in the Levels suited him, and he loved to hear the pop of bubbles to the surface, or the gurgle of a mini-whirlpool by an outlet pipe. He'd see a pike lurking, sinister and predatory, at the bottom of a stream – and would sometimes watch the ensuing drama of hunter and victim, without intervening to eat one himself. The metallic colours of dragonflies, the quacks and croaks and arguments of waders and ducks and herons, the swallows and warblers darting after insects; all these in the moment sights and smells and sounds and impressions began to replace any yearning for a story or an explanation. Sometimes, though, he'd look up from the Shapwick Levels, or West Hay, or Ham Wall, and he'd see Glastonbury Tor and St. Michael's Tower on the horizon, and it seemed to mock him like a one finger salute – telling him that he couldn't just live in the present, that he had to be haunted by stories that didn't exist, by lies and nonsense and empty fantasies. On those occasions he would sit and think and think and think and try to think a hole into the ground – try to summon up the old woman. Where was she? In a circle of naked earth next to Nan Tuck's Lane? Somewhere in the shadow of Chanklebury? In Amberley Wild Brooks? In the Millstone Marshes? Surely the

Somerset Levels would be the place for her – but he couldn't make her appear any more than he could think himself into a hill. And so he'd turn his back on the tor, and fall back into the sounds of water and reeds and birdsong and the drone of insects.

One day, he dozed in the sunshine, and his dreams were a confusing blur of returning stories and the sounds around him. The birdsong mixed with the roar of blast furnaces, crashing cars, the claustrophobia and powerlessness created by the feeling of young men leaning on him or men on board a ship – no power. Then the old woman was giving him a job – watching cakes bake on a griddle – but he was preoccupied with desperate thoughts of his lack of power to concentrate, and the cakes burned. He was a king, a useless king, a powerless king, wounded in the marshes, burning cakes, fearful. And there was an angry old woman, scolding him for burning cakes.

"Don't just sit there on your arse. Get moving. Glastonbury Tor isn't the only tor – west – west – can't you even turn a cake:

Patty Cake, Patty Cake,
Baker's Man;
That I will Master,
As fast as I can;
Pat it and prick it,
And mark with an M,
And there'll be enough for Monster."

Link looked around to hear the flapping of an egret's wings, and a commotion between two crows. No old woman. No cakes. He got up and headed westwards across the Levels.

12: MOON AND MOOR

'Dewer' is the name of the Devil on Dartmoor. He leads the Wild Hunt over the moor, pursuing the souls of unbaptised babies and hunting down evil-doers. He commands a pack of dogs called the Wisht Hounds, huge black dogs with fiery red eyes, controlling them with a whip made from the blackened tongues of gossips stitched together.

Michael Dacre, *Devonshire Folk Tales*

"Brent Tarr is a church on a very High hill I believe nearest heaven of any church in England; the people are very rude and brutish".
Dr James Younge, Devon diarist, c. 1680. (This is a reference to the Gubbins, an extensive intermarried family who seem to have lived in caves in Lydford Gorge, nearby, and had a most barbarous reputation!)

From the website 'Brentor Village; A Dartmoor Community'

Link followed the straight, canalised, Huntspill River across the Levels until the night-time sounds, the calls of waders, the splash of an eel, the screech of an owl, began to be dominated by the increasing noise of traffic.

With the light from the Huntspill Energy Park to his left, the yet-to-be-demolished buildings of the old explosives' factory looking gaunt and skeletal, Link came across a motorway. He wondered where all these people were going in the night. Did they just use their vehicles to randomly hurtle from one place to another? He thought of Guinevere's funeral cortege being rocketed back to Amesbury – then of all the vehicles he'd seen hurtling up and down roads between Piltdown and the Levels. He saw a picture of himself as a solid being in a landscape of whizzing, criss-crossing ghosts. The larva people were pale like ghosts – sitting in their vehicles, ricocheting back and forth along a web of tarmac.

At the motorway he stopped, and thought about his sense of direction, which had been gradually seeping back into him. It was still pulling west, but southerly too. The motorway was going in that direction, so he followed it.

The next day Link was dozing behind some bushes at the top of an embankment beside the M5. He was awoken by the sound of police sirens and watched as a lorry pulled onto the hard shoulder – with a police car in front, and two behind.

He watched the drama – a lot of shouting and arguing – the back of the lorry being opened, and six men climbing out, whilst the policemen milled around them. Link, watching from the embankment, somehow sensed that the men were bone-weary, and had travelled a lot further than he had. He looked at the perspective of the motorway sweeping away south-westward and recalled travelling in a car as a young woman and riding on a dragon steam train as a stoker and wondered about riding in a lorry himself.

The next night he continued to follow the motorway, comforted by the presence of the Somerset Levels on his left hand side. He used the hard shoulder of the motorway to cross the River Parrett, a railway line, and the Taunton and Bridgwater Canal. The moon was waxing gibbous, nearly full in the sky, and Link looked into the canal and examined its reflection. He remembered Lord Moon and spent a night of seeing the moon through trees, and over fields and motorway signs; and feeling that the moon, when it was visible, seemed to be following him. One of his feathers started to glow with moonlight.

Link reached a business park and then the Bridgwater Services. In the lorry park at the service station there was a big articulated truck carrying huge drainage pipes.

Link lodged himself into one of the pipes; not the first time he'd been in a drainage pipe, though usually they were under motorways, and wet and dank and gloomy. As morning came this seemed light and airy, high up on the semi-trailer, though Link felt the need to flatten himself against the inside of the tube; to become shadow. There was a banging of the door as the driver emerged from the cab and wandered off into the services; later another banging of the door before the engine roared into life, and the lorry pulled out of the services; westward bound along the M5.

Link watched a circular, moving picture at the end of the pipe. Mainly he watched sky – blue, with cumulus clouds like mountain ranges – but sometimes he crawled to the end and watched the cars behind, or the cars overtaking, and the perspective of the road curving away behind the lorry. He wondered about all this speed and motion; he was now part of the world that he'd grown used to seeing flashing past; a world that seemed to have no hold on the reality of soil, stone and sand. He sometimes tried to fix his eyes on something static; a large blue road sign. Then it was gone. A hill – one of the Blackdown Hills – it moved more slowly, then faded. The solid became fluid, moving at different speeds. Link marvelled at the difference in speed between objects closer to, or further from, the road.

By-passing Exeter the lorry crossed a wide stretch of the River Exe, before peeling off the motorway, underneath it, and onto the A30. Link crawled to the end of the pipe and looked out, suddenly making eye contact with the astonished driver of the car behind. He rapidly withdrew back into the pipe and remained hidden until he felt the lorry slowing down, pulling off the road, and finally the engine stopping.

There was the sound of the driver alighting from the cab, the slam of the door, and Link peeped out of the pipe into the lorry park of Woody's Diner, just west of Okehampton. Looking up he saw the massif of Dartmoor and immediately felt a pull towards it. His fluctuating memory brought him images of hills rising out of flat land – the South Downs, Portsdown Hill, the Marlborough Downs, the Mendips. There was a pleasure in climbing to a height and this dark, purple massif stirred something in an older memory, a memory that pre-dated this journey. The tips of two granite tors he could see on the ridge seemed to be beckoning for him to climb up to the moor.

He slid out of the pipe and off the lorry. On the far side of the somewhat tumbledown buildings there was a ditch and Link spent the rest of the day there, dozing to a background noise of the coming and going of lorries, voices, slamming doors.

After dark he headed for Dartmoor; through the road tunnel under the A30 dual carriageway, through some woods, then steeply upwards till he was on moorland, rising high and wild ahead of him. He skirted round an army camp, crossed a boggy valley, until he saw the great shape of Yes Tor; a fuzz of moonlight behind it; and a fizz in the air – a sense of buzzing vibration coming from the granite.

The full moon arose from behind the tor and the sight of it was terrifying. It was magnified by the angle of the atmosphere and it seemed to fill the sky; massive, bright, apocalyptic. Link could make out the shapes of craters and mountains and the light seemed to stream out of the moon and into Link's body. He crouched down on the ground, staring in awe up at the tor and the moon and felt that he was shrinking – becoming nothing: unimportant. But this sense of a lack of importance wasn't humiliating. He felt that he was a part of everything: the moor, the tor, all the creatures; foxes, badgers, deer, buzzards, crows – even the larva people, with their frenetic zig-zagging of the land, their perpetual fiddling with everything – building things, knocking them down – their planes and cars and lorries and trains. Link felt that he could almost love them; at least he was filled with the moonlight, the reflected light of the sun, and that was a warmth that felt like love. Then there was a story, he thought, and a sense of desire for something.

Link lost any sense of time, but after the moon had risen higher, and seemed to have resumed a more familiar size, he got up and continued towards Yes Tor.

He usually had a sense when people were nearby: sound, smell, and an acute night vision – and he could slide into a shadow. But this time he was bedizened by moonlight, his mind was just starting to settle down after some sort of a major flux, and he stumbled almost blindly into a group of soldiers.

Their uniforms were torn and carried no insignia. In the exercise they were the fugitives, being pursued across Dartmoor by uniformed and well-equipped soldiers. The exercise was hard and real, there was a sense of fear – but heightened to an excitement, an 'in the moment' feeling of connection, by the knowledge that it was just an exercise.

"Fuckingell", said one of the soldiers. They surrounded Link.

"What the fuck are you?" said another.

Link knew that if he opened his mouth, part beak, and screeched, people fled in terror. He always tried to howl, he wanted to howl, but it was always a squeal that came out. He tried again, but this time it really was a howl – something to do with the sudden imposition of the squaddies onto his former moon-led feeling of connection, as if they were throwing that back as worthless. They were bringing back the claustrophobia of Chanklebury, the bleak nothingness of Glastonbury Tor, and the howl was drawn out long and desolate below Yes Tor.

The soldiers didn't flee; they flung themselves at Link. Link was strong; he could crush someone with his wing; but to be set upon by a whole group of tough men was something quite different. They pinned him down, he flung them off – but then there were lights and the sound of shouting.

It would seem that the reality of the unreality of an exercise had a stronger hold on the soldiers than the reality of fighting a mad mooncalf; and they turned and ran, leaving Link free to fling himself into a mire, from where, through sedge and cottongrass, he watched the pursuing platoon of soldiers, equipped with lights and dogs, pass by.

"You'd think they were the wild hunt", said a voice next to Link, "but them doggies ent wisht hounds". Link turned his head in astonishment and found himself looking at the devil.

"You again", stammered Link after a pause. "Your stitches have been coming undone."

"Eh?" said the devil – "oh, that's not me."

Looking more closely Link saw that this devil wasn't quite the same as his old friend – this devil was that bit more devilish, a sharper nose and chin, a more gleefully demoniacal glint in his eyes – altogether less glum.

"I'm the devil of Dartmoor; Old Dewer they calls me. How do you do?"

"I'm not sure how I'm doing", said Link, who had gone from some sort of internal ecstasy to a fight with a group of squaddies in the space of an hour.

"I'd heard that you were coming" said Old Dewer, "all sorts of hints have been drifting towards me – from that eastern devil, the old woman, the Master of the Stones, Lord Moon, the Burley Dragon." Link felt enormously comforted by this: the thought that he existed in the minds of others, that there was a whole community of the other folk out there who knew about his journey.

"Doesn't look like you've found what you're looking for."

"I thought it was on Glastonbury Tor", said Link, "I went there with Guinevere's funeral cortege."

"Oh, that", laughed the devil, "That's just a lot of old stories. And Glastonbury Tor isn't a proper tor anyway, it's just a pointy hill – bloody sedimentary. You're on Dartmoor now – I can show you a few proper tors."

They climbed out of the bog, Link dripping with brackish bog water.

"That's it", laughed Old Dewer, "can't beat a good scrap – you were well matched against them squaddies. Now I'll show you how to get dry."

Link felt a surge of elation; the transformative feeling he'd gained when gazing at the moon hadn't disappeared with that desolate howl.

"Squaddies and dogs", shouted the devil, "I'll show you dogs." He put two fingers in his mouth and whistled; a shrill whistle that spiralled up the valley, and a great, black horse came hurtling downwards, through the air, from Yes Tor, followed by a pack of huge hounds in full cry. Their eyes shone red and sparks flew from the horse's hooves.

Old Dewer mounted the horse in one easy movement.

"Come on, mooncalf", he roared, "up behind me." He hauled Link up onto the horse and they all shot up into the air. Link was exhilarated – the baying of the hounds, the sound of the devil blowing on a copper hunting horn, the shower of sparks trailing through the night sky.

They hurtled, and veered, and helter-skeltered across the moor, dodging and skimming Yes Tor, East Mill Tor, Oke Tor, Hound Tor, Hangingstone Hill, Fur Tor, Rough Tor, Great Mis Tor, North Hessary Tor (spiralling around its transmitting station mast), a moon-led, sky dancing, visual poem of a night ride.

"What are we hunting?" shouted Link.

"What – what? Oh, that's a good point."

They circled down, into the centre of the moor, coming to rest in Wistman's Wood. Link slid off the horse, which promptly shrank, turning itself into a black rat, and settled between mossy stones, amidst short, stunted, oak trees, whose twisted branches and trunks presented a strong feeling of witchery.

"I like to base myself here", said Old Dewer and, looking round at a ribbon tied to a branch, added, "It's getting like your bloody Glastonbury here, bloody people looking for their inner selves and littering the place." Link didn't know whether he was looking for his inner self, though he was looking for something, and he felt embarrassed.

"Occasionally I give one of them a fright, but it's not like the old days. Them's the days when I'd send a thunderbolt down on Widecombe Church, and claim a soul or three, the days when I'd play cards for the soul of a squire, when I'd do some real hunting, and chase some bastard over the moor, wisht hounds a howling, till he tumbled off the edge of the Dewerstone. Then the real old days, before all that – when I'd stand on top of a tor, waving me vitals around, and they'd all worship me. Nowadays, I don't know what they're all about – buzzing around like bees in a hive – but without the wit to make honey."

"Can you stitch up wounds?" asked Link politely, like…"

"…my brother. No need for that; we're in Wistman's Wood."

Old Dewer was more angular, and sharper, than the devil of Tunbridge Wells, but his healing skills seemed so much more gentle. The mosses and lichens of Wistman's Wood were cool and damp on the frayed and severed stitches, and Link felt skin melting into skin, and moonlight filtering into his body through his feathers. He remembered marching down from the Mendips, seeing the mosses of Ebbor Gorge, but being in too much of a hurry to feel their coolness. Now he relaxed. Relaxed with the devil.

"So, if it's not Glastonbury, where are you going?"

"I want to find Tadig Kozh – it's a church, or a tower, on a hill."

"That'll be Brent Tor", said the devil, casually.

Link looked at him sharply.

"You know it – you know where Tadig Kozh is?"

"Who?"

Link felt a surge of disappointment.

"Brent Tor sounds like your place – but the name Tadig Kozh sounds Cornish."

"Breton", said Link, "I believe he comes from Brittany – is that Cornish?"

"Well, sort of – let's go to Brent Tor."

The black rat appeared on top of a moss-covered boulder and blew itself up into a great black stallion again; the wisht hounds bayed.

"Mount up – away we go." Up into the air again, and like Guinevere's funeral cortege they were only visible to those people who see such things – up and over Black Dunghill, Cocks Hill, White Tor – between Mary Tavy and Peter Tavy, and then Brent Tor was ahead of them.

Link felt that his heart seemed to physically leap within his body when he saw Brent Tor. There was a familiarity about it, the church on the rocky basalt outcrop at the edge of the moor. It looked right.

With the devil blowing his horn, the horse trailing sparks, the hounds baying, they circled the tor three times, then landed right in front of the door to the church. The devil blew it open.

"Is this the place – where is your Tadig Kozh?" And then Old Dewer abruptly withdrew.

"There has been someone here", he said, with what, to Link, seemed like the most surprising look of fear on his face. "Someone who can settle devils. No doubt someone who can stitch together monsters", he added, looking at Link.

Link looked into the church – spare and simple, though dominated by the stained glass picture of Saint Michael on the window over the altar.

"Saint Michael" said the devil, "killing dragons on hills – bastard."

Link ventured into the church. It felt familiar, almost something like home. He too sensed a presence. He remembered a hand reaching down and pulling him out of Chanklebury, and he felt that sense of aid and care here. He lay down, waiting to sink into the hill, but nothing happened. There was no feeling of failure and desperation this time, though. He felt that this was just a hill that he wasn't going to sink into – but, unlike Glastonbury Tor, it held a significance for him.

He walked out of the church.

"Well", said the devil, "Are you any the wiser?"

Link wasn't sure. He felt his sense of direction shift southwards.

"I don't know. I think I may need to go south now."

"South – poo – you'll end up in poxy Plymouth. If Tadig Kozh is Cornish – Breton – you need to go west. The old church here, before the 1300s, was a chantry chapel; a place to pray for the souls of the dead. Plenty of them drift around here with the Dartmoor mist, so I reckon you need to go to the Isles of the Dead. West, west. West to sunset, where the souls go. Out to the islands. Where old Sulis drops into the sea."

"Can I ride there with your wild hunt?"

"To the Isles of the Dead, don't be scilly. I'm on Dartmoor for ever and a day; or at least till I'm not here anymore. The Isles of the Dead are hardly a place for me – not till I'm ready."

Link felt a sense of déjà vu – talking to the Burley Dragon about the route to Amesbury.

"Just go west till you fall off the end. No, go to the end of the alphabet, turn the story into a reading book – go to Z. Go to Zennor – find the mermaid. She'll take you there. Oh yes, I'm sure she will. In the morning, not long, look west, and you'll see Bodmin Moor. Head for that. Granite to granite. One moor to another, then keep west – Penwith. To Zennor. She's in the church. Sun'll be coming up soon, I'm off."

Before Link could say any more, ask any questions, even say goodbye – there was a woosh and hounds, horse and devil hurtled off eastwards, back over the moor, towards Wistman's Wood.

Watching them disappear, Link could see the haze of light in the east, as the sun began to rise. Looking westward, as the darkness slipped away, he began to make out more wild land, way away on the horizon – a distant blur of granite and deep moorland green. He descended the western side of Brent Tor and took shelter in a patch of woodland in a fork in the road, two narrow, minor roads, so straight that they looked Roman. Throughout the day, between sleep and dozing, Link could hear the clatter of helicopters over Dartmoor.

13: THE MERMAID OF ZENNOR

Dozmare Pool (pron. *Doz'-mary*)...It is the traditional scene of the 'passing of Arthur' (see Tennyson); the giant Tregeagle is condemned to empty it with a limpet shell. In winter it supplies large quantities of ice.

C.C Ward, *Through Guides: North Devon and North Cornwall*, 1908

Schoolgirl discovers mystery sword in same lake King Arthur's legendary Excalibur was thrown. Seven-year-old surprised to find four-foot blade lying underwater.

***The Independent*, 5th September, 2017**

Nellie Sloggett (29 December, 1851 in Padstow, Cornwall, UK – 1923) was an author and folklorist who wrote under the names **Enys Tregarthen** and **Nellie Cornwall**.

Wikipedia

The Mermaid of Zennor (Cornish: *An Vorvoren a Senar*) is a popular Cornish folk tale that was first recorded by the Cornish folklorist William Bottrell in 1873. The legend has inspired works of poetry, literature and art.

Wikipedia

In a mile or so onward we reach **Zennor** (*Pub.-ho.*). The church (restored) is early 13th century, and interesting; the font, Late Decorated, is good, and there is a curious bench-end representing a mermaid. Nothing can well be rougher than the granite strewn surroundings of the dilapidated village. A logan-stone, capable of being rocked, is just north (?) of it.

C.C Ward, *Through Guides: North Devon and North Cornwall*, 1908

The next night, with the moon following him, Link set off westwards, towards Bodmin Moor. Once again there was the sound of traffic, and once again he was following the A30.

Over the next few days the moon waned, and Link walked – left to right, left to right, foot and claw, foot and claw. The claw was flat now, like a bone plate, and when Link walked on tarmac, which he mostly avoided, it went clack – clack – clack. Sometimes Link wondered whether he could climb onto a lorry again, but the opportunity didn't present itself and he continued to walk. He had renewed strength, though, and he fell into a rhythm. He felt that the Isles of the Dead were somewhere ahead, and that there was a target, whether that was a tower or a church on a hill, or Tadig Kozh, or death and the dead, he didn't know; but there was a target.

During one night's walking Link heard a screech of brakes, followed by a thump. Then there were voices, and the sound of a car moving on. Emerging from trees, Link saw a fawn lying in the road, its guts spilling out onto the tarmac. Link approached it, thinking of food, then saw the doe, its mother, nibbling grass at the verge. She looked sharply up at Link, and then jumped back into the woods as a motorbike approached. The headlight of the motorbike picked out the body, and the bike swerved round it, the rider only just managing to keep control. It roared on. The doe appeared at the woodland edge again, trotted out to her fawn, and sniffed it.

"You're next", thought Link, "one of those cars or something will hit you." He walked, awkward clip-clop gait, out onto the road, the doe jumping back into the woods, caught hold of the body by its hooves, and pulled it into the trees. He moved away, and the mother returned to her fawn, and continued to sniff it. Spilled blood and tangible reality, thought Link – whilst the larva people flash by. He felt that moon flooded sense of love again but suffused with an overwhelming sadness.

"Why did this bloody Tadig Kozh stitch me together?" he thought. "Keep walking. Keep walking."

13: THE MERMAID OF ZENNOR

The road climbed into the wide, open country of Bodmin Moor. Link kept close, until, seeing the buildings of Jamaica Inn, he headed towards them to find some human food scraps. Round the back of the buildings Link felt his sense of direction pulling south, setting up a tension between that and his desire to head due west. He allowed himself to walk south-west and away from the road.

Link saw a still, grey lake ahead and approached Dozmary Pool. A creature, long, black, feline and fluid, flowed through a gap in the stone wall.

"You're the Beast of Bodmin Moor now", said the Lady of the Lake, "it might as well disappear back to its zoological theme park". Link felt the warmth inside that characterised his encounters with the other people; the old woman, the devils, Trivia, the dragon.

There was a dilapidated fence, wire on wooden posts that led down into the lake, continuing until it disappeared into the water. Link sat on the patchy grass next to it and watched the Lady of the Lake wading towards him, one hand on the fence. She looked like a more human version of the marionette Guinevere, though rather damp, and, in spite of being draped in a diaphanous dress, not at all cold.

"You're not Lancelot" – Link was jolted by a sudden, sharp, memory of Guinevere shouting "Lancelot, Lancelot, kiss me no more".

"Are you Griflet? – Gruffle, snuffle, Griflet – come to throw Excalibur into the lake?"

Link gazed at her blankly.

"Maybe you're Arthur himself." The name "Arthur" made Link think about desolate wanderings around Glastonbury, and he felt a brief wave of depression.

"I don't understand you", he said.

"Someone threw the sword in here", she said, "and I caught it. The last time it was some strange bloke from Redruth, who wore army trousers, though you'd never get into the army with a pony tail and a belly like that. I let a little girl find it – seemed right."

If Link hadn't understood her before, he understood even less now.

"Isn't Arthur buried at Glastonbury?" he asked. "Guinevere's funeral cortege keeps trying to go there, but they get shot back to Amesbury."

"Oh, that's just a lot of old stories", said the Lady of the Lake. "The monks at Glastonbury wanted to bring in the pilgrims – tourists – call them what you will. Arthur's here, on Bodmin Moor, buried under Brown Willy. Where he belongs."

Link resigned himself to not knowing what the hell she was talking about.

"We've got lots of stories in Cornwall, because vicars collected them up, mainly vicars, and wrote them down. It's a funny reason for having stories if you think about it. I mean people make stories, like Tadig Kozh made you. I know all about that."

At the mention of Tadig Kozh, Link tried to interrupt but, without needing to raise her voice, the Lady of the Lake was impossible to interrupt – the onward flow of her speech was relentless.

"… but some old vicar comes along and writes them down, at least his version of them, and suddenly they're 'proper' stories, and they get written down again and again. I got written down in folk stories by vicars, and by authors in their endless 'works of art', and mystic, shmystic bollockses, and novelists and poets and the rest. I wave a sword around, flash my tits a bit; and all those blokes, those painters and poets, start dribbling and sighing. Repulsive if you ask me. And then along come the feminists and give me 'agency', as if I never had it in the first place. Why can't they all piss off and leave me be?"

Link could only gaze at her in complete perplexity, as she carried on, hardly leaving time to take breath – though maybe when under water she didn't need to.

"Mind you, you could weave all your aches and pains into a witch's ladder. What vicar wrote that one down? The Reverend" … she said "Reverend" in a very disrespectful tone… "Sabine Baring-Gould – funny how so many of the men who write about me have got double-barrelled names – but he didn't write about me. It was the witch's ladder, all wool, string and cock's feathers; and you stitch your aches and pains and ailments into it, and fling it into the pool, and they all float away. You'll have a few aches and pains..."

Link tried to mention his battered claw, and his aching wing that couldn't, on its own, get him to fly, and the body that ached from the imbalance of foot and claw, and arm and wing; but she wasn't listening – and on she went:

"Well, that's just another story. Oligotrophic, this lake, you know. Do you know what that means? Most people don't. Low in nutrients – though it can support me. Mind you, it lost a lot of the creatures it had when they flooded the valley and made Siblyback Reservoir. That was an upset. Not great for a Lady of the Lake is it; having a reservoir nearby, sort of spoils the image. Nellie Sloggett – now she was the one for the stories. They called her 'the little cripple'. She lay in bed in Padstow and dreamed the countryside around her into stories. Then people went in and told her tales. Collected lots; piskies and such – mermaids."

On hearing the word 'mermaid', Link braced himself and bellowed over the ever increasing tide of verbosity:

"DO YOU KNOW THE STORY OF THE MERMAID OF ZENNOR?"

"Oh yes – of course." She stopped.

"Old Dewer told me she could help me find Tadig Kozh."

"That one was collected by the Reverend William Bottrell. He collected the most. I expect he flowered it up a bit – they usually did. Why?"

"Old Dewer says she could get me to the Isles of the Dead."

"Oh, she could do that all right. Yes – dead."

"Pardon?"

"Well there's the Isles of the Dead, and just being dead. You have to watch her. But yes, Arthur floated off to the Isles of the Dead on a beautiful boat in those stories, with me watching over him, being all diaphanous and floaty and such like. As if.

They're the Scilly Isles – why don't you just catch the boat? It's called the Vomit Comet, sails from Penzance."

"Can you just get on a boat – like all those people who …?"

Link didn't know how to describe the people, the larva people, the people who weren't the other people – the other than the other people. He paused, and this time she didn't fill the gap with her own word torrent … "who are real."

"THE PEOPLE WHO ARE REAL!! What ARE you saying? Would you deny your own existence? You smell real enough. Don't people sometimes see you?"

Link thought of his scrap with the squaddies, of making eye contact with a driver on the A30, of being spoken to by a woman on Glastonbury Tor, of bursting out from behind the bins in an Amesbury car park, of a car hitting a roundabout, of a cyclist in Tunbridge Wells. He thought of a man with a story to be told on Farlington Marshes – and he felt a sense of shame.

Far away, in Worthing, a young man stared at a computer screen and drew a line from Glastonbury to the A30 on the Devon-Cornwall border.

"…but no, I can't just get on a boat. I spend all my time here, catching bloody swords – or handing them out. It's worse for him…"

Link looked to where she was pointing, and saw a scowling man trying to ladle water out of the pool with a colander.

"He's Jan Tregeagle, one of Baring-Gould's – made a pact with the devil. Never mind Old Dewer, there's a few devils on Bodmin Moor. But your Mermaid of Zennor. She might be able to help – but you'd really have to have your wits about you. She's not interested in the fate of others. Never was. There's real peril there. Do you know the story?"

"No, I don't, that's why I asked?"

"Oh well, Mathey Trewella sang in the choir – lovely, tenor voice. Would move your heart strings. His voice would echo out from Zennor church, Saint Senara's, and over Pendour Cove. Well, one day a lovely lady came up the steep path from the cove to the church – no-one knowed who she was. She came up three times – well, it has to be three if it's not seven – and she gazed at Mathey and he gazed at her. The third time he followed her down – disappeared – never seen again. One time a boat was sheltering in the cove from a storm. They dropped anchor and a mermaid pops her head out of the water and tells them off for dropping the anchor at the mouth of her cave, blocking in her husband and children. Lovely story. Mathey Trewella 'took the tail' ... became a merman. People go to the church, and there's a carving of her on a bench end, and they can listen to the booming of the sea below the cliffs, and think of the story, and get a distant look in their eyes – and people put it in books and plays and poems, and there's lots of them, and it's ever so lovely, like me. I'm lovely. Diaphanous – like I said – I do like that word. I float from the lake and I prefer to catch swords in slow motion, and Arthur floats over to the Isles of the Dead, and I stand over the body and look beautiful, and the Mermaid of Zennor grows legs under her dress and walks gracefully into the church leaving a trail of seaweed and salt water, and we waft – we waft."

"Please" said Link, desperately interrupting, "please. Will she take me to Tadig Kozh? Is Tadig Kozh on the Isles of the Dead?"

She stopped and gazed at Link.

"I don't know. He's somewhere around. Cornwall. Brittany. Same really. The Isles of the Dead. None of us can go there, or we wouldn't be here. The Mermaid of Zennor is likely to take you somewhere, even if it's just a cave under Pendour Cove. Have you got a good singing voice?"

"What?"

"No – I doubt it. She's probably your next guide – but watch yourself. A guide doesn't necessarily have your interests at heart."

The Lady of the Lake gestured back towards the main road.

"Follow the big road, the one they've splatted over the moor. They've been widening it forever. Follow the piskie hats."

Link knew what she meant by piskie hats, he'd seen plenty of traffic cones.

"Don't hang around on the moor or go wandering off to the coast; you'll drown in stories. Follow the road, west all the way, until you get to a hill from where you can see both coasts, south and north. Then follow the north coast into the third moor – Dartmoor, Bodmin Moor, Penwith is the third – and walk to Zennor."

She followed the fence back down into the lake.

"Good luck" she shouted, "Think of me when you meet Tadig Kozh; stories."

Then she was gone and Dozmary Pool was still and silent. Link looked around for Jan Tregeagle, but he was gone too. The black, feline shape flowed through the gap in the stone wall, and Link turned his face south-westwards to the A30.

Link spent the next night walking past JCBs and a whole variety of heavy-duty road construction machines, past cranes and caravans and endless traffic cones, past road junctions to minor roads blocked off by concrete blocks and barriers, where the roadworks spilled out onto the moor. Finally there were no roadworks, just the great westward sweep of road leading off the moor, but still over the open land of that central spine of Cornwall.

During the day Link dozed behind the Cornwall Services at Roche, hidden in a ditch, almost in plain sight; but when people leave the main road for a service station their immediate world is delineated by the boundaries of that service station and its connection to the road – for them it isn't part of a wider landscape, and anything beyond those boundaries is just a blurry backdrop. A small open-top truck pulled up, without going onto either car park or lorry park, and two bearded young men, arguing with each other, got out and opened the bonnet. On the back of the truck was the strangest object, shaped like an onion, the bottom of it like a globe, but at the top a long pipe.

Link remembered his ride in a large pipe on the back of a lorry and wondered about this. It was a mash tun that the two young men were transporting to their new micro-brewery, but to Link there was the possibility of another ride along his westward route, but not quite such an openly inviting container. Whilst the young men argued, and fiddled incompetently with the spark plug leads, Link climbed onto the back of the lorry, and lowered himself head first into the mash tun – a claustrophobic squeeze, wing and arm crushed to his sides, and a wriggle downwards into the dark globe. Then he stood up, unbending himself, and fortunately for Link he was just tall enough for his head to poke out of the top of the tube. There was a bang as the bonnet was slammed shut, and Link quickly withdrew his head back into the mash tun.

The engine spluttered into life, and they jolted off. Every so often Link would poke his head out of the neck of the mash tin and rotate like a periscope. Drivers behind didn't know what to make of this, but most didn't recognise the mash tun for what it was, so something odd rotating on the top didn't make it seem any stranger. Link watched the open country as the road cut a direct swathe through the Newlyn Downs, avoiding towns and villages, until the truck left the main road, and headed into the built-up area of Hayle. It pulled up at a bus stop and Link, in a pantomime of wriggles, watched by an astonished old woman from the bedroom window of a terraced house, eased his way out of the mash tun, dropped to the ground and disappeared into some back gardens.

Two policemen had a cursory look through the back gardens but failed to see Link hanging upside down from the branch of a tree, hidden by branches and leaves that were beginning to turn yellow. Night fell rapidly because dark clouds were gathering as the light of the sun faded. The wind picked up, and a maritime shower whipped across, exhilarating Link, who dropped from his tree and headed west, skirting the edge of the Hayle Estuary. He was pushing against his sense of direction now, which seemed to be wanting to take him south and east – but the desire to head west was stronger. The words of Old Dewer and The Lady of the Lake, the thought of the Isles of the Dead waiting, the prospect of a guiding mermaid – all pulled him westwards, to continue what he had done for miles – to head for the setting sun. Not that there was any setting sun visible that night: he walked in darkness, damp with windblown showers that were filled with the smell of the sea. He ascended the hill that lay ahead of him, Trecrobben, and stood on the pile of granite boulders on the summit, arm and wing outstretched, feeling the wind and the rain tear through feathers and skin and fur. Around him, through the sound of the elements, he could hear tinkling sounds; stones being rolled in the wind, or a thousand spriggans spilling out of the rocks, dancing and fighting – whilst somewhere the Reverend Bottrell wrote down a tale and Nellie Sloggett, confined to her bed, dreamed the surrounding landscape into stories.

The next day he hid a little further down the hill in bushes, but, being a blustery, wet day, no-one came walking up there, so Link went to the top. A shower swept over, and briefly the sun shone and clouds rolled away. Link saw coast, both to the north and the south, where he saw St. Michael's Mount, before more clouds came rolling in. St. Michael's Mount had been like a vision, and Link wondered if it could be his destination. With his sense of direction pulling him southwards, and a building on a hill and an island beckoning to him, Link found it difficult to head north-westward towards the north coast. It's what the Lady of the Lake had told him to do, but she did go on and on. But then it was as if all these other folk – the devil, the old woman, the people of the stones, the Burley Dragon, Old Dewer, even Lord Moon – were waymarkers and he shouldn't ignore them.

He reached the coast and the cliffs and felt both fear and excitement to hear the booming of the sea, the thud as a wave entered a cave, and then roared back out again. At Pendour Cove he saw signs of a village up above and felt a strange nervous fluttering inside himself. He thought maybe he'd reached the place the Lady of the Lake had told him to go to and seek the mermaid. He sat by the cove and listened to the sea. Over the thud and the boom and the surge, he heard another sound – the sound of a great chord, made up of bass, baritone and tenor, then, as a surge of the sea was thrown back by the land, the chord became a broken discord, before settling back into harmony as another surge came rolling in. Link stayed there throughout most of the day, but in the late afternoon, impatient with waiting, he headed up towards Zennor.

13: THE MERMAID OF ZENNOR

There were a few people about, but Link was able to avoid them as he eased himself over the wall into St. Senara's grave yard, looking up at boulder-scattered moorland hills that loomed over the old church. The door was still unlocked, and Link entered a seemingly empty building. He saw a model boat hanging from the ceiling, and then in a side isle there was someone sitting on a bench. Link didn't feel his usual instinct to hide when he saw a person; this felt like someone waiting for him. She wore a long green dress.

"I am beautiful" she said. Link looked at the veil that covered her face and thought of the compound eye of a fly.

"Mirror and comb" she said, "They said that's my vanity – I tempt men with my lust and vanity."

Link remembered something that the devil had said about Saint Dunstan and original sin.

"Do I tempt you?"

Link thought of another life, hazily imagined from a more distant past than his appearance in Piltdown. He thought of steamed up cars in Tunbridge Wells, he thought of couples having sex in the bushes whilst he tried, hidden, to remain asleep. He didn't know how to answer.

"Hah – you're no Mathey Trewella. And their story – my mirror and comb and power. The mirror is a knuckerhole."

Link remembered clinging on to a knucker, spiralling through cold water.

"They attach their temporary beliefs – see it the way that suits them at the time."

She pointed at the carving on the end of the bench, the mermaid chair on which she sat. "Someone cut a slice across my breasts" – there was a gash across the carving; a slice – "That was disapproval at the time. Mixed with lust of course; isn't it always? But you reach into a story, you hack at a story, you change it. The story isn't just something outside yourself."

Link looked at the face in the carving. It was blank, flat, featureless; where generations of hands and fingers had touched it. The remains of the mouth was a slit.

"Can people change the story by touching the carving?" he managed to ask.

"What's a story?" she said, "People, humans, can't just respond – they can't just breathe, hunt, flee, copulate, eat, drink, shit, be born and die – they're too weak. They have to make stories – they have to try and explain. It's how they survive. Until they die. Then they're dead."

She laughed – a snigger of a laugh.

"So they change stories themselves – when they rub my face into nothing, when they shove their grubby fingers through the worlds, they rub my face into nothing. Where are you going?"

"To find Tadig Kozh. Maybe on the Isles of the Dead?"

"Interfering old priest. Isles of the Dead? You want a bit of shining oblivion?"

She lifted her veil and her face was blank except for the gash of a mouth.

The horror Link felt wasn't based on aesthetics – well, what did he look like? It was because there was something in the blankness that made him think of the loss of stories, something he'd felt in Glastonbury, something about nothing – a terrible void."

Then the head of an eel shot out of the slit-mouth and needle-like teeth attached themselves to Link's face. He squealed a pig squeal and wrenched it off. The eel shot back into her face, and she hissed in his ear: "I'll tell you a story – I took Mathey Trewella down into the cove, down under the water. I tore his throat. I ripped out his vocal cords to string a bone harp. I have them all down there. They sing to me. Can you sing? Can you sing? Can you only squeal like a pig?"

"Howl" spluttered Link, "I can howl" – and he howled, as he had done on Dartmoor – a howl that picked up a sympathetic resonance from one of the church bells, and echoed out over the Giant's Rock and Pendour Cove, up the hill and over the moor to the Logan Stone and Zennor Quoit.

"I want that, I want that", she screamed, and with Link clasped in her arms she rocketed out of the church door, and, like a whirlwind twister, the two of them, locked together, spiralled down the slope to the sea. Link struggled against her vice-like embrace, pushing her blank face, and the eel's head, away. They hit the sea hard, like a diving gannet, and as they dived down Link felt the strain from his battered claw and his calloused foot fade away as his lower half transformed into a fish's tail – he felt strong. The eel clamped its needle teeth onto his throat, as they hurtled between bone harps set upon killas, pillars of metamorphic rock.

Struggling, wrestling, they spiralled further out to sea, accelerating all the while – hurtling around a Russian nuclear submarine that was as agile as they were. Then, beneath them, there was the city. Towers and pillars, seaweed flags, shining palace of shell and bone, barnacle encrusted houses of sea washed drift wood.

Another mermaid hurtled towards them from the city – beautiful and terrible as, surely, a princess amongst mermaids must be.

"Mermaid of Zennor" she bellowed, "This one isn't yours."

"You want this one?" said the Mermaid of Zennor. "You wouldn't want this thing for your bed chamber. Let me have his vocal cords – they can howl."

"They wouldn't blend into any chord you'd want" said the princess amongst mermaids. "Leave him be. He's on a journey – and I'm to help him, not kill him."

"Pah – bloody stories", said the Mermaid of Zennor and shot away in a stream of bubbles.

"Well", said the princess, "Welcome to Lyonesse, or Ys, as some call it. You've been having a hard time. Do come in."

14: MOR BREIZH

Agrippas are living, malicious creatures, and resent being read. An untamed agrippa will display only blank pages. To get the letters to appear, the agrippa must be battled, thrashed, and beaten like a stubborn mule. A fight with an agrippa can last hours, and victors come out of it exhausted and drenched in sweat. When not in use, an agrippa must be chained to a strong, bent beam.

Brittany, A Book of Creatures
https://abookofcreatures.com/category/brittany/

The main thing to note here is give yourself plenty of time. Many instruction sets will give you an idea of how many people and how long it should take but not all. Two sections below indicate:
How long it should take
Typical Tools Required
General Assembly Tips.

Online instructions for putting together flatpack furniture

The princess brought Link to a chamber, where mermaids applied various seaweeds and squelchy, squishy stuff to the gashes and bite marks around his throat. From the waist down he was all fish tail, and that felt fresh and comfortable, though there was an echo of the ache and pain of foot and claw within it. There was no sign of stitches: the upper part of his body was shaped as before, though covered with smooth, shining scales, and gills amidst the abrasions on his neck.

The princess introduced herself as Dahut and told Link that she was princess of Lyonesse and Ys; two names for the same place, the one name being Cornish, and the other Breton.

"Because a country has a river running through it, that doesn't turn it into two countries", explained Dahut, "and this country has a bit of a sea, a channel, Mor Brettanek, Mor Breizh, running through it, but it is still a country, and the sea is the main part of it. Lyonesse and Ys are one."

Link wanted stories, but it seemed rude to say, "Once upon a time?" He was being treated with such courtesy and respect that he felt such a request would sound like a demand.

"Am I a mer… man?" he asked haltingly, "or am I a mermonster?"

"Monster", she said, "is a word applied by others, I've been called 'monster' often enough. I think you are more man than any other creature that is part of you, and a mighty fine merman you are too."

Link had never blushed before, but he felt himself turning bright green. He tried to mumble something about her being a mighty fine mermaid, which sounded like a very lame response. "I think 'maid' is not a term to be applied to me – I'd rather be known as a merwoman", she said with a smile. Link, unaware of the nuances of speech of the land-based larva people, or their sometimes apoplectic resistance to rational change, thought this a perfectly reasonable request.

"My mother was a Korrigan, a sea creature, and my father was King Gradlon, King of Cornouaille, and you can put that on either side of the Mor Breizh, though his court was in Quimper. I stayed in the more ancient city of Ker-Ys, though they had to build a great wall around it to keep out the rising sea. They say I was wicked, or they say I'm exciting. Or they say I was wicked, but secretly find me exciting. Or they say I'm a goddess, and a fine example of independent womanhood, or they say this and that, and play their harps and tell my story. They say that I put hoods over the heads of men, and took them to my bed, and in the morning I strangled them. They say the devil shagged me, but I couldn't strangle him, and he took the key to the sluice gates and let in the sea…" Link had a vision of the devil of Tunbridge Wells and didn't think he'd have much of a chance against the Princess Dahut. "Whatever the story, the sea was coming in, and my father, who was in Ker-Ys said, 'jump up behind me on my horse, we must race the waves to the shore', and we galloped and galloped whilst a great wave chased us. But the voice of Saint Gwenole, the great Christian, said, 'Save yourself, throw your daughter from the horse, then you can outrun the wave', and so my father threw me from the horse, and the wave engulfed me and Ker-Ys, and I became a Korrigan like my mother, a merwoman."

Link was horrified. He thought nothing about interpretations of the story – pagan, Christian, new-age – that was all blaaah to him; all he saw was a father throwing his daughter from a horse in order to save himself. Had this happened to him? If Tadig Kozh had constructed him, was Tadig Kozh his father? Had he abandoned him in remote Piltdown? Was that any different to Gradlon hurling Dahut from his horse? Did he want to find this man?

"Your father should not have done that", Link stated simply.

"My daddy – my tadig kozh – my old daddy."

"Tadig Kozh? Your old daddy?"

"Just Breton for old daddy, you'll see, you're shifting between their languages. But I know who you're talking about. Tadig Kozh, the old priest with the Agrippa. Come with me, come to the feasting. We'll discuss this at the table."

She brought Link to a mighty hall, with walls of shining shell and quartz, and a great table of slate, inlaid with Cornish tin and with legs of pink Breton granite. Sitting at the table were a variety of creatures, amongst whom Link didn't look particularly strange. There were crustaceans, fish, molluscs, marine mammals, creatures like anemones that seemed more vegetable than animal, combinations of all the above, mermen, merwomen, mercattle, korrigans, morrigans, kelpies, selkies, seals, dolphins, sea-horses and gulping blobfish. Link was brought in and seated, in as far as he could be seated, at the head of the table next to the Princess Dahut. Link was overwhelmed; he'd never been treated like an honoured guest before.

"How can I introduce you to those assembled here?" asked Dahut.

Link looked at her blankly.

"What is your name?"

"I have none. The devil called me a Piltdown Man, the old woman and Lord Moon have called me monster."

"I will not call you monster – all of us here can be called that."

She turned to the assembled multitude. "Ladies and Gentlemen; cryptids of the ocean; we have here a cryptid of the land, a cryptid we believe to have been constructed by Tadig Kozh of the Menez Bré…". There was a murmur, or perhaps a gurgle, from the diners. "He has temporarily 'taken the tail' on his crossing through Lyonesse and Ys and has graciously consented to visit and honour us with his presence."

Link felt hugely embarrassed and turned bright green again.

"He has fought off the Mermaid of Zennor – but will he seek to fight me off, tonight in the royal bedchamber?"

The crowd roared, trumpeted, gulped, guffawed, blew bubbles, and clapped fins. Link felt a great surge of alarm.

"Would you like to say a few words?"

"Th… fr…" Link tried to say something, but just blew bubbles which whirled away in confusion.

"No need, no need. Come let us eat."

During the meal, Link asked the Princess if the Isles of the Dead were his destination.

"The Isles of the Dead are only for the dead. When Cornish people looked west towards the setting sun, looked in the direction that you have walked for all these miles, they saw the Scilly Isles and they paddled westwards with their dead. In Brittany they paddled to Ushant or the Ile de Seine, where the morrigans live. But a place is a place – a place in the mind. If you make it real – geography – you forget, like people always do, that a story is the way we survive, it is our method, not our goal."

Link didn't follow, but it worried him.

"But Piltdown is a place – geography. And isn't the Menez Bré?"

"Ah yes – they are – we reach through the worlds, just as all those fingers reached through and rubbed the face of the poor Zennor mermaid into blankness, and so it is that you are making a journey, maybe even a pilgrimage. You are telling the tale with your foot and claw, or your rather fine fish-tail. I don't think the story, the journey, has an end, though."

"But I hoped the Isles of the Dead were the end, or is it the Menez Bré? I need to find Tadig Kozh – he who made me. Him and his instruction manual."

"...and then what?"

Link had never considered that. He thought of walking as something superior to mere thinking, juggling words: "Then I find out."

"Find out what? That there are no stories? Tomorrow we will send you back to the land, so you are near the Menez Bré. From Ys you usually come ashore at Finisterre but we'll take you down the coast to the Lieue de Grève, where Arthur fought the dragon."

Arthur again.

"This Arthur, King Arthur, is he real?"

"I doubt it. He's a story and he's lots of stories. At the Lieue de Grève there was a dragon living in a cave...", Link thought of the Burley dragon and wondered if it could turn into a steam engine. "It had one red eye in the centre of its forehead, its shoulders were covered in green scales, its long powerful fish tail was black and twisted, and its vast mouth was furnished with tusks like a giant boar. It was terrorising the neighbourhood, as they do, and Arthur, having defeated the dragons of Wales and Cornwall came to do battle with this one."

"Did he cover himself with birdlime and broken glass?" asked Link.

"I imagine that's another story", Dahut replied patiently, "let me tell this one."

"Sorry."

"At first Arthur didn't know that the dragon was at home, because the dragon always went into the cave backwards, making his footprints look like he was out. So the dragon came charging out, catching Arthur unawares. The battle raged for three days and three nights – no-one had got anywhere, the dragon dragged itself back into the cave, and Arthur collapsed to the ground. Well, who should come along but St. Efflam."

"Who?"

"St. Efflam. An Irish prince who gave it all up to become a holy man. Sailed to Armorica – Brittany – on a millstone and became a hermit. Well, anyway, he raised his mighty staff, uttered a few incantations and shouted, 'Thou spawn of Satan, in the name of God I charge thee to come forth'."

"God?"

"Ah, now there's a story."

Link remembered something about a jealous God who had thrown the devil out of heaven, so that he landed somewhere on the South Downs, but it was too much to absorb, so he didn't ask any more.

"Roaring and hissing like a thousand serpents, the dragon dragged itself from the cave, and, whilst vomiting forth fire and blood, climbed the Great Rock, Le Grande Rocher which overlooks the whole league of beach, he shrunk to a tiny size, trotted down the hill, and became St. Efflam's very own, teensy-weensy, little tame dragon.

St. Efflam has given his name to a little village at the end of the Lieue de Grève, and from there it's not too far to the Menez Bré. Tadig Kozh has walked those lanes many a time, and depending on what world you're in, the traffic isn't as bad as you're used to in England."

"Tadig Kozh" said Link, "please tell me about Tadig Kozh."

"He was a priest… of sorts. Maybe he was around before St. Efflam and the rest of them came sailing across on their millstones, carrying their dragon-slaying religion with them. He was always old and scruffy, though his face sometimes looked like that of a child. They called him Tadig Kozh, little old daddy. He could cure ailments, take the black depression away from people, sing a good song, tell a story, take a drink; and he was a great one for interpreting the Agrippa."

"The Agrippa?"

"A book – sometimes farmhouses had one chained to a beam in the cellar – huge books; they told how to summon and banish devils, how to cure farmyard diseases, how to ease rheumatic pain – some say how to create life – the middle two were the most important for Breton folk."

"How to create life. An instruction manual?"

"I suppose so. There are many stories about him. One tells how a soldier returned from the war. He was nearly home when, passing the Menez Bré, he met Tadig Kozh, accompanied by a big, black dog.

'Tadig Kozh', says the soldier, 'good to see you after all these years – do you know me? – I'm home from the wars.'

'Good to see you', says Tadig Kozh. 'Your old mother will be overjoyed to see you again. Now, on the way home you will be passing the rectory at Louargat. Will you give this dog to the rector there? I'm old and tired and want to walk no further.'

So the soldier did so, but the rector recoiled.

'Look at its eyes', shouted the rector, 'it's a devil. I can't deal with it. Take it to the rector at Pédernec, I don't want it.' So the soldier takes it to Pédernec – same thing. 'Take it to Bégard' – then it's 'take it to Pluzunet', then it's Trégrom, then it's Belle-Isle-en-Terre, where the rector says take it to Louargat, which would have taken the soldier widdershins around the Menez Bré. So the soldier takes it up the Menez Bré, to the chapel of Saint-Hervé, and who should be there but Tadig Kozh. Turns out that the dog is the soul of the soldier's own devilish grandfather and Tadig Kozh has to say a midnight mass backwards and read from the Agrippa, in order to banish the soul to the place under the hill."

Link stopped following the story when he heard about the chapel of Saint-Hervé, a church on a hill. He sensed an ending to his own long journey.

"Now, my dear cryptid, enough of this storytelling. I have got the most wonderful bedchamber – there is a tradition. Would you accompany me there?" Her smile was crooked and rather irresistible.

Link looked down at his tail, and thought of the larva people steaming up cars, or ploughing away doggy fashion in the woods. He felt his face glowing green again; "You mean, have sex?"

She laughed at his naïve directness; "You're used to the land animals, my dear. It's easier for fish."

Link wondered whether he was being asked to perform a task, like singing for his supper. Was this some spontaneous joy – or a demand? It felt like something that was required of him, just to enable his crossing from Cornwall to Brittany. He was also tempted, fascinated, nervously excited, and he gazed at Dahut's great, undulating tail, as he swam behind her.

Below the waist, he was all fish tail himself.

He followed Dahut into her bedchamber, feeling nauseous with a mixture of fear and anticipation, and he saw the great bed of seaweed, the lamps of shell and narwhal ivory, the Ikea garden lanterns that the tide had swirled out to sea from the remains of a beach barbeque.

"Spawn, dear creature", she breathed, amidst a swirl of particularly elongated bubbles. Link felt an intense twinge of pain and pleasure in his fish tail and, with a sense of release, emitted a cloud of fish milt that floated downwards towards a similar cloud sloshing forth from Dahut, who, writhing with pleasure, gave off a semi-tuneful moan, like a whale – which is most definitely a mammal.

Link gazed at her, and was about to ask, "Was it good for you?", but the words seemed to drift away from him. Fortunately.

"Settle down, dear Piltdown fishman", she breathed. "Sleep now; one spawning is enough for a night – a damn sight more than a dozen human couplings."

In the morning – under the sea Link had abandoned his nocturnal existence – Link was bedizened and bedazed, and didn't really want to leave at all, however close he felt to his destination. Dahut, however, was matter-of-fact, almost indifferent, and Link felt his sense of rejection returning.

"We need to find you transportation", she said brusquely. "Follow me."

He swam behind her to a compound that was piled high with millstones.

"All originally made for grinding corn", she said, "not a function they can perform very successfully under water – not that they have much function on land in the nowadays days anyway – purely decorative. They do love their nostalgia."

She looked from one millstone to another, sizing them up with an expert eye.

"The old saints in the stories used them for transportation: Ireland to Brittany, Brittany to Cornwall, Cornwall to Wales. The sea was full of their saintly sailings. Nowadays mermaids use them; they're neat little forms of transportation – very nifty."

She gestured to a rather unctuous seal attendant, "Fetch me three mermaids who are competent with transportation and navigation."

"Yes, your ladyship", said the seal, bowing deeply.

He returned with three mermaids. They had impassive faces, and bright, blue, stone eyes.

"Take that one", Dahut gestured at a millstone. "It looks reliable. I think reliability is the main thing here; nothing too sporty. I'm sure our Piltdown Man here doesn't want anything too dangerous or exciting." She glanced at him, and Link, thinking of the previous night's activity, suddenly wondered if he'd been a great disappointment, and once again flushed a deep green.

"Go on then, Piltdown Man, climb aboard. Sit in the middle, dangle your tail through that central hole there."

So Link did and the millstone lifted off the sea bed and started, slowly, to revolve. As it revolved upwards, Link looked at the Princess Dahut, wanting a response – a farewell – but she had already turned tail and was swimming away, towards the palace.

15: LE MENEZ BRÉ

Sing Riwal, the wizard Riwal,
The satirical bard
Riding a broomstick
To fly on the Sabbath.
And the crowd of demons around him
Screaming through the fields
And the black dwarves of the hill
Trained in their crazy round
And porpoises with long grunts
And the sea horses who neigh
On the top of foaming waves
When the storm roars and roars the thunder
And the beautiful siren so treacherous
Half woman, half fish
Who seduces sailors by her songs
And makes the ships break against the rocks.

From *Les Bardes de Cambrie* by Prosper Proux – with a little assistance from Google translate. The poem is about a sorcerer who lived on the Grand Rocher, near St. Efflam.

On reaching the surface, Link saw a blue sky and a calm sea, as the millstone set off in a south-easterly direction. Link's sense of direction, which had been changing since entering Cornwall, felt much more satisfied.

The mermaids remained impassive and silent, and their shining, stone eyes made them look both vigilant and sightless. Link looked down for his tail, but it was gone – a foot and an ungainly, flattened claw dangled in the water. On his body the gills were gone and the shining scales had all disappeared. He felt a deep sense of disappointment.

"Can I no longer be a merman?" he asked the mermaids. They ignored him.

That morning Link saw a passing oil tanker, the Roscoff to Plymouth ferry, a large container ship and three yachts. The millstone and its strange crew were not seen by anyone on board the ships; they were just a story. A blur of coast to the south slowly moved into focus and Link saw a wooded hill and a wide, wide stretch of beach. In the centre of the strand, looking tiny amidst an expanse of sand, a dot – a figure.

The millstone ran aground amidst lapping waves, and Link jumped off, relishing the feel of shifting sand beneath his foot, and a tickling around his claw. The mermaids stared blankly at him with their stone eyes, so he pushed the millstone off the shore, and watched them float back out to sea.

He turned again and watched that dot of a figure, centred within the vast beach. They approached each other gradually and, as the figure grew clearer, it slowly came into focus as a stern-faced man, dressed in black, woollen robes. Link watched the man's eyes focus in on him, and the man's expression changed from stern, to angry, to rage.

"Thou fiend from hell", bellowed the man, "though monster sent by Satan – in the name of almighty God, I command thee to kneel before me."

Link's own bewilderment turned to anger – he'd had enough. Was this Tadig Kozh? The man who had made him and then abandoned him. If so then Link was going to take no abuse.

"Fiend from hell yourself", shouted Link, "Who do you think you are, commanding me to kneel? I could crush you."

"I am Efflam – servant of God – and you are an abomination."

As Link lunged forward, the mighty saint lifted his staff.

"In the name of Christ the king...." Link had him by the throat "......shrink, devil, shrink", spluttered the saint.

And so Link did. He shrank and he shrank, till he was a fraction of his former size, and as he did so, something seemed to sit upon his mind, something soft but heavy, something suffocating and deadening, and it compressed his mind, and put a heavy blanket over his thoughts, so that all he knew was that he had to be obedient to the mighty Saint Efflam.

The saint rubbed his throat and gave the little Link a kick.

"Follow me, you are now a servant of God" ordered the saint. So Link followed him, across the beach towards woodland and the hill.

At the foot of the hill was a great rock, Le Grand Rocher. The saint entered his hermitage, his cave. Bats hung from the ceiling, looking like upside-down, miniature versions of the saint himself. Saint Efflam pushed Link unceremoniously into a small adjoining cave and slammed an iron grill shut behind him. Link could give no reaction, no response. He just gazed blankly at the miniature dragon that appeared to be sharing the little cave with him. The dragon hunkered down, belly to the ground, ears back, and shivered, like a chastised dog.

In a dull, mindless state, Link stayed with the saint for several days. He and the little dragon would stare at each other in mute misery but were unable to share a sense of fellow feeling, their thoughts being crushed by the saint's power. They weren't even able to squabble over the few scraps the saint threw to them, but would sit and gaze at the unappetising food till one or other darted forward. Sometimes the saint would come to the grill and deliver long sermons, and the sonorous words felt, to Link, like the beating of a sock full of sand against his head.

Every so often the saint would put a lead around Link's neck and take him walkies to a little chapel situated westwards along the shore. Sometimes he took the dragon – the saint showed them off to a glum congregation. Link did what he was told, as did the cowed little dragon.

Then one day, he woke up in the cave to hear the voices of children and the sound of a car driving past. Link felt the possibility of something but was unable to shift his mind – to think of the possibility of inhabiting different worlds, to wonder why the saint's cave was empty of his bits and pieces. He looked at the dragon, who shivered in a corner.

A couple of hours passed, during which Link heard cars and passing voices, and then the daylight, just visible from outside the main cave, started to fail. There was a scraping and snuffling, and a dog's nose appeared under the iron grill. The dog's eyes were a piercing yellow. Link touched the dog's wet nose and it growled. He looked at the dragon, and in his mind's eye, he saw a steam train. "All aboard – all aboard" said a voice in his head, then he had a vision of a dragon spiralling out of a hill and up into the night sky.

Link looked into the dog's eyes and heard Old Dewer give a yell and a tally-ho, as the wild hunt rocketed over Dartmoor. He flapped his wing, as he felt his body start to expand, and caught hold of the iron grill and pulled at it.

He was fearful at the way his body was expanding, soon it would be too big for this little cave within a cave. He saw the dragon and himself being crushed, dying amidst terrible compression and claustrophobia.

"Wake up, wake up" he shouted at the little dragon, and the great black dog barked, a deep, booming, woof. The dragon shook itself and burped. It too started to grow. Link hauled desperately at the grill, trying to force his wing into the gaps, so he could pull with arm and wing. The dog scrabbled harder.

Then the dragon belched and puffed out a breath of smoke. He burped again, and then blew a stream of fire out at the grill. The dog yelped and jumped back as Link hastily withdrew his hand and wing. The dragon blew fire again, aiming at the padlock. Link and the dragon were now completely wedged into the tight space, the shackle on the padlock glowed white hot and the dragon poked it with a claw. It clattered to the ground. Link and the dragon, which was now the size of a Shetland pony, squeezed out into the larger cave, and dragon, dog and cryptid danced around in a circle, roaring and howling and barking. They emerged from the cave, past the 'defense de fumer' sign, and out into the evening. The dragon puffed itself up to full size, shot up into the sky and was gone in a trail of sparks.

15: LE MENEZ BRÉ

The dog jumped up at Link, barked, and then set off along a track through the woods, up the slope of the Grand Rocher. At the top Link could see the lights twinkling around the bay from the Beg Douar to the Beg ar Forn. He breathed in the sea air, looked round for the dog, and Saint Efflam stepped out of the trees.

"Foul fiend", he roared, raising his staff. The dog galloped past Link, leaped into the air and grabbed the staff in his jaws. The saint bellowed; "Give me my holy staff, cur", and the dog dropped his head and the forward part of his body to the ground, tail wagging, and let go of the staff. The saint rushed at it, the dog grabbed it again, galloped off, and dropped it on the far side of the glade. Once again the saint ran forward, once again the dog took the staff to the far side of the clearing, where he wagged his tail, barking furiously at how much fun the game was. The next time the saint rushed at the dog, the dog disappeared into the trees. Saint Efflam pursued him into the woods, then Link heard a growl and a scream, after which the dog returned, looking a lot less playful, but very satisfied. He looked at Link, then set off in a south-easterly direction, down the southern slope of the hill, towards the church tower of Plouzélambre, visible in the autumn twilight, as they emerged from the woods.

It was a rapid night-time run, as Link lumbered, his strange jolting, uneven run, after the dog. Sometimes he lost it, and the dog would run back and bark. There were fields and walls and fences and woods – a standing stone, sunken lanes, a raggedy moon. They skirted the sleeping village of Plouaret, briefly followed the River Léguer, and dashed across the E50 autoroute, a road whose distance was a journey that was many times further than the one Link had made – a route from Makhachkala in faraway Dagestan, to Brest in Brittany. To Link and the dog, however, this was not a route, this was a slice of tarmac, an obstacle made dangerous by hurtling vehicles. A startled Parisian lorry driver and a book dealer from Guingamp caught a glimpse of the pair in the head lights. The book dealer pulled onto the hard shoulder, partly to recover from the shock of a near collision and partly to try and process what she had just seen.

15: LE MENEZ BRÉ

As the sun rose in the east, Link and the dog settled down for the day in a sunken lane, an ancient track once used by people and carts, now a green holloway, near Belle-Isle-en-Terre. Link caught a glimpse of a hill in the distance, with a building on top. His heart skipped a beat, but he was exhausted and slept throughout the day.

The next night they crossed the E50 again and headed towards the church tower at Louargat. They passed it and Link had a clear view of the Menez Bré against a moonlit sky. He felt the jolt that he had felt on seeing Brent Tor, but this time the certainty that this was his destination. Link started up the hill, but the dog growled and fastened its jaws around his leg, dragging him back down. Link kicked the dog away and it leaped between him and the hill, barking and growling. Link remembered the story that the Princess Dahut had told him, of the soldier and the dog and Tadig Kozh.

Widdershins – widdershins – widdershins.

His whole mind screamed at him to ascend the hill, go up the Menez Bré, head for the church on the hill, but he thought of the story, of finding Tadig Kozh – the dog was obviously a guide – he must follow it.

On they went to Pédernec and a frustrated Link saw the hill fade into the darkness, then on to Bégard, the town of the bear, further again from the Menez Bré, but north, they had looped round the hill. The dog padded, and Link limped, through the deserted streets of the night-time town, and then on to Pluzunet, further still, north-west, from the hill. They settled down in a fragment of woodland next to a stream – then as morning came, and Link looked longingly towards the Menez Bré, a hare broke cover and the dog pursued it across a field. During the day they feasted on hare, tugging and pulling and growling at each other. The next night, amidst the screech of owls, they headed across fields and fences and ditches towards Trégrom.

They reached the E50 again, with Belle-Isle-en-Terre on the other side, and Link realised that they had completed a widdershins circumambulation of the Menez Bré. He turned towards the hill, away from the autoroute, and they walked and stumbled and trotted across the fields and upstream along a tributary of the Léguer that was more ditch than stream. North of Louargat the dog stopped and growled and, with a suddenness that left Link standing, shot off up a holloway.

Link started up the holloway, pushing through brambles and branches, till behind him he heard a rattle and clatter. Clattering impossibly through the thick vegetation, came a rickety cart pulled by two emaciated horses. Sitting up on the cart was a figure dressed in black, with a wide-brimmed hat. The figure was clutching a scythe, on which the blade appeared to be attached the wrong way round. Link stood directly in front of the cart, wing and arm by his side, and it clattered to a halt in front of him. The face of the carter was shaded by the brim of the hat, but he appeared to be regarding Link, as Link regarded him.

The carter reached out an arm. Link walked to the side of the cart and, catching hold of Link's one arm, the carter hauled him up, so that Link was seated next to him. The arm that pulled Link up onto the cart was the arm that had hauled him out of Chanklebury.

"As for the cart, its base was made of a few loosely fitted planks; two rude hurdles served as sides. A great gawk of a man, who was just as scraggy as his beasts, led this pitiful team. A large felt hat shaded all his face."

Description of the Ankou, transporter of the dead, from a story told by Marie-Yvonne of Port-Blanc to Anatole Le Braz, and written down by him in *Legende de la mort en Basse-Bretagne, croyances et usages des Bretons armoricaines*, 1893. Translated by Derek Bryce.

Link looked into the face of an old man, a face that looked both ancient and childlike.

"You made me", said Link.

The carter grunted.

"You made me, speak to me."

The cart rattled on further. Link looked behind to see a pile of corpses in the cart, dressed in dark suits, black dresses and tracksuits. Shackled to the leg of one of the bodies was a huge book.

"I put you together", said the carter, after a while. "There was all those bits and pieces lying around; it was a shame to waste them. Those charcoal burners died alone; there was no priest out in the forest to say words over the bodies."

"Do they need words?"

"They needed stories, they needed something to put their existences into order. I took the parts and gave them more stories. And you. And the badger and the crow and the wild boar."

"Why did you make me?"

"I needed something to do."

Link had thought that if he met Tadig Kozh, he would be angry, filled with rage. But, on being hauled up onto the cart, all that anger had faded away. Now, however, he felt it return.

"That's no answer – why did you make me?"

"I don't owe you explanations", said Tadig Kozh, as he turned towards Link, his eyes blazing. Link saw the yellow eyes of the black dog.

"You do."

"Think it enough that you exist. Why you exist is just a foolish question – a human question – a cruel idiot thinking that there's something real in stories."

"Isn't there?"

"A fox needs cunning and teeth to stay alive. A rabbit needs powerful legs and fear. People need stories. Ways and means."

Link could make no reply, because Tadig Kozh halted the horses and climbed down from the cart. He removed his shoes, placed them in the back of the cart amongst the dead bodies, and, putting his scythe over his shoulder, took hold of the bridle of the leading horse, and led horses, cart, Link and corpses on up the hill.

They rattled to the top of the hill, and the old chapel of Saint Hervé stood in front of them.

Link and the carter entered the church, and Link was strongly reminded, in its simplicity, of the church of Saint Michael, on Brent Tor. Saint Michael though, like Saint Efflam, was a dragon slayer; Link felt that Saint Hervé would be no such thing.

In the corner of the church there stood a statue of a Breton knight. Link regarded it solemnly as Tadig Kozh stood at the altar rail.

"Come, my cryptid, come and stand beside me – you are part of the Ofern drantel."

16: THE OFERN DRANTEL
(The Mass of Trentaine)

In the old days, it was the custom to have *thirty people* celebrate each other, that is to say, a series of thirty services. The priests said the first twenty-nine masses at their parish church. But the thirtieth, it was customary to go to the chapel of Saint Hervé, on the summit of Menez-Bré. It is this thirty-year mass that the Bretons call *Ann ofern drantel.*

It was celebrated at midnight. It was said backwards, beginning with the end.

On the altar only one of the candles was lit.

All the deceased of the year went to Mass; all the devils also appeared there.

The priest who was going to say it had to be at once very learned and very bold. From the bottom of the mountain, he took off his shoes and climbed the slope barefoot, for he had to be 'priest to the ground'. He was going up, holding a silver clam with one hand, waving a brush with the other, and continually sprinkling on all sides. Often he had difficulty in advancing, so much was he around by the dead souls, eager to receive a few drops of holy water, and thus to obtain a momentary relief.

The day before, he had carried in the chapel a strong bag of flax seeds.

Mass said, he began the call of the devils,

In the porch. They ran, shouting, wild screams. It was the terrible moment. Woe to the officiant, if he lost his head! He silenced the demons, paraded them one by one, forced them to show their claws to see if the soul of the deceased, for whom he had celebrated the *ofern drantel,* had not fallen into their possession, and then returned them to measure, distributing to each one a seed of flax, for the devils never consent to go away empty-handed. If he committed a single omission, he was compelled in exchange to deliver his own person. He therefore incurred his eternal damnation.

Anatole Le Braz, *The Legend of Death in Lower Brittany,* 1893. Translated, in inimitable fashion, by Google translate.

The chapel door creaked open and the corpse with the book chained to its leg came shuffling in, dragging the great book behind it.

"The Agrippa", said Tadig Kozh gravely and, after unshackling the book from the corpse's leg, signalled to Link to pick up one side of it, which, using arm and wing, he did.

They propped it against the altar and the carter, the Ankou, the old priest, Tadig Kozh, opened it.

He started to intone the words and the statue of the Breton Knight groaned and then clattered out of the church doors. He returned followed by the corpses from the cart, all shuffling along in single file. They sat themselves down on the pews and the knight resumed his position in the corner.

"Come; come up out of the hill", bellowed the priest; and a bearded man dressed in a dark suit rose up through the flagstones.

"Tis I", boomed the man, "Anatole Le Braz, holder of the stories, the Bard of Brittany."

"Wait for this", said the priest sideways and sotto voce. There was a roar and a bellow, and a raggedy man appeared from the ground – "I'll 'ave you, you thieving bastard", he roared at Le Braz, "You stole my stories – folklore my arse. Look at this – church and priests – I hate the lot of them. Give me my stories, you literary piece of shit."

He pursued the terrified looking Le Braz around and around the inside of the church.

Link looked enquiringly at the priest.

"That's Jean-Marie Déguignet; he thinks Le Braz stole his stories. Always a dangerous business, collecting other people's narratives – he didn't really intend to steal anything."

"Oh", said Link.

"The story goes on. These things don't just sort themselves out in the afterlife."

The priest, unperturbed by the racket being made by Déguignet, continued with his intonations.

Next up came a whole squabbling procession of folklorists and writers and storytellers and folk who believed that their stories had been stolen and altered, and they shouted and screamed at each other, and accused each other of plagiarism, and Link, looking at the Agrippa, saw them all dancing and leaping and hobbling in the illuminated pictures, and he saw monks painting the pictures in a scriptorium, and he saw people telling stories in parlours and fields and boats.

The figures in the illustrations mirrored the figures capering around the church, and then sometimes changed, so as Link looked around him, and at the book, he started to confuse all the different images. Then there were dragons and mermaids and ghosts and goblins and banshees and trolls and piskies and korrigans and knuckers and wisht hounds and on and on and on – and then the men with the hi-viz jackets from under Hag Hill.

BANG!! Tadig Kozh slammed the book shut, and the figures were all gone. Link looked round at the corpses sitting in the pews.

“This is tiring work”, said the priest, “and I must give them all communion. Let’s have some refreshment first.”

He sat down on the altar step; “Come, sit beside me”, he said to Link, and reaching into his cloak, drew out a bottle of cider. He tried to pull the cork out with his teeth, but then swore and muttered that he didn’t have many teeth left.

“Here, you get this cork out”, he said to Link, handing him the bottle. Link locked his teeth onto it – or was it beak? – and hauled the cork out with ease. He handed the bottle to Tadig Kozh, who took a deep swig, and then the old priest handed it to Link, who did the same.

“Did you hear the story of how I met the devil on the road to the Menez Bré?” asked the priest.

“No”, said Link, who after the hullabaloo liked the idea of settling down with a bottle of cider to a good story.

“Ah no, I’m in the middle of the Ofern drantel, better be getting on with it.”

The priest stood up, and, facing his congregation of corpses, continued with the mass. They all stood up and waited in a line along the aisle, whilst the first one knelt at the altar rail. Tadig

Kozh reached beside the altar and produced a dusty bottle full of a dull red liquid, and a box. He handed the bottle to Link.

"You give them the wine, and I'll give them the wafers."

Link didn't know what to do.

"Go on, give that poor fellow a swig."

Link presented the bottle to the kneeling corpse's mouth and it took a sip. Tadig Kozh put a wafer into its mouth and said the words. The corpse gave a great shout and rocketed up through the ceiling.

They continued with this, some of the corpses hurtling through the ceiling, some sinking into the ground, until there were no corpses left.

"Now for the non-fiction", said the priest.

"That was irony you know", he said to Link, who didn't know what he meant.

He opened the Agrippa and next out of the hill came scientists and researchers and technicians and physicists and alchemists, and they argued and screamed at each other and accused each other of plagiarism and insisted on the authenticity of their own stories, and rushed and rushed around the church, whilst Tadig Kozh continued intoning and chanting, and the illustrations in the Agrippa mirrored and contradicted the circling figures, and sometimes figures leaped out of the pictures, and sometimes they leaped into the pictures – and there was a gabbling of voices, and the larva people driving cars, and mechanics looking at manuals, and there were people lost in giant shops, and flat pack furniture, and instruction manuals.

INSTRUCTION MANUALS.

Link tried to reach for one with his hand, but his arm became a wing, and he had two wings. The whirl around him was a blur. He saw the ancient, baby face of Tadig Kozh – "Go up", shouted the priest, "Up up – take narrative out to space – infect somewhere else with the virus."

Link flew up through the chapel roof, and wings outstretched, spiralled up into the sky, a whirl of dragons and mechanics and lab technicians and farmers and mermaids and characters from narrative and holders of narrative behind him. He spread his great wings and gave a great crow-like caw of pleasure, gazing out over the lights and towns of villages from the coast to the Mountains of Arrée. As they spiralled on upwards, a golden figure from the whirl and swirl of figures shouted, "Icarus, Icarus – the story of Icarus." A story flashed through Link's head like an electric shock, and he started to fly back downwards, through the cloud of narrative that reversed its shape, like a jellyfish sinking into the sea.

He floated back down through the roof of the chapel, and sat on the altar step next to Tadig Kozh, who was eating a crêpe, and taking swigs from the cider bottle. Link's two wings had become two arms.

"Why did you make me?" asked the cryptid, who no longer looked like a cryptid.

"There you go again", said the priest. "Have another swig of cider and sit awhile."

So they sat and drank that bottle and then another.

"Here, help me with the book", said the priest, after a while. Tadig Kozh and Link took the book through the door of the church and out onto the cart. The priest shackled it to an iron ring that was bolted onto the side.

"This could be a small book you can take into the bookshop in Guingamp", said the priest. "Or it could be a story you tell to a young man who's stuck to his computer screen in Worthing. You could add the story of the man in Farlington Marshes; there are many that are worse. Take care of the dead, my friend, I'm going under the hill."

Then Link found himself, two feet and two arms, reversed scythe over his shoulder, broad brimmed hat on his head, sitting on the seat of a cart pulled by two emaciated horses.

"I'll feed them better" he thought and, feeling under his cloak found two bottles of cider. He geed up the horses and they started to clatter down the Menez Bré.

Bibliography

Baring-Gould, Sabine, *A Book of the West,* Methuen & Co, 1899

Bottrell, William, *Traditions and Hearthside Stories of West Cornwall, Volume 2,* 1873. Reprint by Llanerch, 1996

Chandler, John, *The Vale of Pewsey,* Ex Libris Press, 2000

Dacre, Michael, *Devonshire Folk Tales,* History Press, 2010

Déguignet, Jean-Marie, 1834-1905, Translated by Linda Asher. First published in French 1998, *Memoirs of a Breton Peasant,* Seven Stories Press, 2012

Le Braz, Anatole, *La Legende de la mort en Basse-Bretagne, croyances et usages des Bretons armoricaines,* 1893, translated by Derek Bryce for Samuel Weiser, Inc., 1999

Malory, Thomas, *Le Morte d'Arthur,* originally published by William Caxton, 1485

Meynell, Esther, *The County Books: Sussex,* Hodder and Stoughton, 1937

O'Leary, Michael, *Hampshire and Isle of Wight Folk Tales,* History Press, 2011

O'Leary, Michael, *Sussex Folk Tales,* History Press, 2013

Staines, Revd E. Noel, *Dear Amberley: A guide to Amberley and History of the Parish,* Amberley Parochial Church Council, 1968

Tregarthen, Enys (pseudonym for Nellie Sloggett), *North Cornwall Fairies and Legends,* Wells Gardner, Darton & Co., 1906

Ward, C.S., *North Devon and North Cornwall,* Thomas Nelson and Sons, 1908

Acknowledgements

Thank you to Phil Smith aka Mythogeography, for his generous support and encouragement, and for his company on a drift or two.

Thanks to Andrew Carey and Triarchy Press for support.

Thanks to my son Danny for getting me Jean-Marie Déguignet's *Memoirs of a Breton Peasant* because it looked interesting, and he thought I might enjoy it. I did.

Thanks to whoever it was who was briefly picked out in my headlights as they lurched across the road in Piltdown one night. Best wear hi-viz if you're going to do that in future.

About the Author

I have been a professional storyteller since 1995; this means I am more used to *telling* stories than writing them. For me, telling a story is more fundamental – the exchange between people, the swirl of patterns and motifs underlying the words, the effect of sounds and smells and light and dark as the story is being told, the questions and changes taking place that make each storytelling session different. I remember being told fragments of stories about hollow hills and sleeping warriors on a farm in Fife during the 1950s, when I was a small boy. It isn't just the focus of the story I remember, but a warm breeze, the smell of hay, and the Doppler effect sound of a jet aircraft as it flew into nearby Leuchars aerodrome. My writing, though, attempts to explore the telling. There may be a contradiction in that.

I worked as a greenkeeper and a gardener before taking a degree, mainly focused on geomorphology. Afterwards, in my forties, I became a primary school teacher. Becoming a storyteller seemed to be to adopt the only profession for which all those things could be considered an apprenticeship.

I have lived in Southampton since 1978 and remain there, possibly more out of inertia than anything else. We don't always choose where we end up and where our roots go down – and when we try to we invariably kill the place we thought we loved. Southampton chunters along, it functions, and I feel the locality. I wander away from it frequently, though, and talk to people, and listen to them, and gather up fragments of stories, and wonder why we do it – why we string experiences together to create narrative.

My job, being a storyteller, involves words and music – and told stories are not separate from, not contained in a different box than, a song; there are repetitions, choruses, rhythms.

I can be found on **www.michaelolearystoryteller.com** and on Facebook: **@MikeOLearystoryteller**.

About the Publisher

Triarchy Press is a small, independent publisher of books about bringing systems thinking (noticing the context, seeing the bigger picture) to:

- organisations and government, financial and social systems
- daily life: moving, walking, performing, art, culture, ecology, gardening.

Triarchy Press has published a number of books about radical, performative or alternative walking (by authors like Roy Bayfield, Alyson Hallett, Ernesto Pujol, Claire Hind, Clare Qualmann and Phil Smith) as well as post-fairy tales like this book and *The MK Myth*. For details of all of them, please visit:

www.triarchypress.net/walking

Lightning Source UK Ltd.
Milton Keynes UK
UKHW020444120219
337161UK00005B/173/P